I

wanna

Be

where

you

Are

I Wanna Be Where You Are

KRISTINA FOREST

Roaring Brook Press • New York

Published by Roaring Brook Press
Roaring Brook Press is a division of Holtzbrinck Publishing
Holdings Limited Partnership
175 Fifth Avenue, New York, NY 10010

fiercereads.com

Library of Congress Control Number: 2018955874

ISBN: 978-1-250-29488-3

Our books may be purchased in bulk for promotional, educational, or business use.
Please contact your local bookseller or the Macmillan Corporate and Premium
Sales Department at (800) 221-7945 ext. 5442 or by email at
MacmillanSpecialMarkets@macmillan.com.

First edition, 2019
Book design by Cassie Gonzales
Printed in the United States of America

1 3 5 7 9 10 8 6 4 2

For my mom and dad

Chapter 1

For the Greater Good

Here's something you should know about me: I'm a terrible daughter.

"For the thousandth time, Chloe, you are *not* a terrible daughter," my best friend, Reina, groans on the other end of the phone. "We've talked about this, remember? What did we say?"

I lie back on my bed and stare at the poster of Avery Johnson on my ceiling. It's a still of him as Prince Siegfried in *Swan Lake.* He's wearing white tights and a white tunic with gold and silver trimming. His brown skin is shiny with sweat. His knees are bent and his arms are outstretched, waiting for Odette, the beautiful white swan, to waltz toward him. I've spent countless nights staring at this poster, dreaming that it was me he would twirl in his arms. And now that the opportunity to meet him is finally here, I'm lying on my bed, frozen, because I'm terrified to lie to my mom.

"Chloe," Reina prods. "What did we say?"

I sigh. "We said that the plan is for the greater good."

"Right, so put your mom on the phone. I'll pretend to be my mom, and I'll tell her you're staying at my house for the week *like we planned*. You'll go to your audition and she'll never know the difference."

I roll over and cover my face with my pillow. "But what if it doesn't work?"

Reina gasps. "Are you seriously doubting my natural-born thespian talent?"

"I don't mean that," I say. Reina takes being an actress *very* seriously. She's a chameleon who can be anything, anyone. I've witnessed her imitate her mom's Dominican accent more times than I can count, so I have no doubt she'll be convincing. "I mean, what if we're lying to her for no reason? What if I get to the audition and I freeze up, or I get lost on the highway, or I forget to put on deodorant and my armpits stink every time I lift my arms, or—"

"CHLOE." Reina's voice cuts through my downward spiral. "Put your mom on the phone or you can kiss your dreams of being a professional ballerina good-bye."

That makes me jerk out of bed. "Hold on."

I walk to my mom's room and take a deep breath before I open her door. I never lie to her. Ever. I've never had a reason to. I'm a girl who goes to school, goes to dance class, has only one best friend, and watches YouTube clips of ballet performances from the 1970s for fun. I don't even have a curfew because *I never go anywhere*. I especially never drive alone to another state for a dance audition without telling my mom.

This is a mistake. The worst idea I've ever had. In the dictionary, you will see my photograph right next to the word *idiotic* because—

"Hey, baby," Mom says, opening her bedroom door. "Do you have Reina's mom on the phone?"

"Yes." My voice is high-pitched like I just sucked helium out of a balloon.

"Okay." She looks at the phone in my hand, waiting. Quickly, before I can change my mind, I place it in her palm.

"Hello?" Mom says as she presses the phone to her ear. "Yes, hi, Camila. I'm doing well. How are you?"

I let out a shaky breath. Mom walks toward her bed, and I follow her, stepping around the open suitcase and clothes strewn across her floor. This morning she's leaving for a week-long cruise with her boyfriend. This is nothing short of a miracle. The only time Mom ever leaves New Jersey is when she's taking me to ballet class in Philadelphia.

I sit on the edge of her bed as she crouches down to throw more clothes in her suitcase. "I don't want Chloe to be a burden to you," she says to Mrs. Acosta/Reina. "I'm really grateful that you're letting her stay with you while I'm away." She reaches up and pushes her long braids out of her face. They're so tight that if she moves her head too quickly, she winces in pain. She usually wears her hair in a short Afro. I walk over and tie her braids into a ponytail. She smiles at me gratefully.

I feel another pang of guilt, and I turn away because I'm afraid she'll know something is up just by looking at me.

It's April and this week is spring break. Mom thinks I'll be spending it around the corner at Reina's house. Reina is actually spending the week working at a kids' theater day camp, and today I'm really auditioning for a spot with Avery Johnson's ballet conservatory, a preprofessional dance school for teens. I'll spend the rest of the week at home, most likely replaying the audition over and over in my mind. Although the audition is in Washington, D.C., the conservatory is in New York City, a city that Mom would never let me live in by myself. To be honest, I don't think she'll ever let me live anywhere alone. No matter how old I get.

I don't want to lie to her, but I have to. Last month, Miss Dana, my ballet teacher at the Philadelphia Center for Dance, pulled me aside and showed me the conservatory audition schedule.

"You need to be there, Chloe," she said, pointing to the New York City audition date. She leaned forward and lowered her voice. "If you do well, there's a chance they'll offer you an apprenticeship with the company."

Me, Chloe Pierce, a seventeen-year-old Black girl living in the middle of nowhere, New Jersey, could spend all of senior year in New York City, learning from Avery Johnson, the youngest Black dancer to start his own ballet company, and now his own conservatory? And afterward, if I was offered an

4

apprenticeship with the company, I'd be one step closer to becoming a professional.

"And thanks to a few generous donors, the conservatory is offering scholarships to everyone accepted in its first year," Miss Dana continued. "Your mom won't have to pay a cent. You should take this chance, Chloe."

I looked down at the scar on my left ankle and felt doubtful.

"You've trained so hard these past few months," Miss Dana went on. "You've got to do it."

She was right. There was no way I would pass up auditioning for Avery Johnson.

It's too bad Mom wasn't on the same page. She wasn't excited about the audition. Instead, she tried her best to conceal a horrified expression when Miss Dana spoke to her after class.

"New York City isn't really in our plans," she said.

Miss Dana looked as disappointed as I felt. She'd trained me for this moment since I was thirteen. She tried to convince Mom that this was a once-in-a-lifetime opportunity. The conservatory was only for high school students. I wouldn't be able to audition next spring, as a senior. But Mom wasn't swayed.

"I'd really appreciate it if you could help Chloe look into some college dance programs," she said. "Maybe at some of the colleges nearby."

College? Why would I want to go to college when I could

be a professional ballerina? Why would I waste all the time I spent working so hard? All the physical therapy and tears.

"But—Mom—" I stammered. My mouth opened and closed like a dying fish's.

"No," she said firmly. And that was that.

Miss Dana slipped the schedule into my hand as Mom and I left. "In case she changes her mind," she whispered.

But I knew Mom wouldn't change her mind. She has her reasons for wanting to keep me close. My dad died in a car accident when I was three years old, and I think she has this irrational fear that something just as terrible will happen to me. It doesn't help that a year and a half ago, I nearly got hit by a car and ended up with a broken ankle. After my ankle healed, Mom almost didn't let me come back to ballet because she thought I'd be under too much pressure. Her tendency to be cautious had never really bothered me until I realized she definitely wouldn't let me move to New York City alone, even if it meant my dreams would be crushed.

A few nights after the New York City audition came and went, I sat on my bed and stared at the Avery Johnson poster on my ceiling and wondered why I even bothered going to ballet class anymore. When I started to cry, something weird happened. The poster fell from the ceiling and drifted right into my lap. It looked like Avery was staring up at me, telling me it was going to be okay. The next morning, Mom's boyfriend, Jean-Marc, surprised her with a vacation, and to everyone's surprise, she actually agreed to go. I took it as a sign.

Avery Johnson and his team will be holding auditions in different cities this week. D.C., Raleigh, Atlanta, and all across the country. Once Mom and Jean-Marc leave today, I'm driving to the Washington, D.C., audition.

"Knock, knock." Jean-Marc pokes his head in the doorway just as Mom ends her phone call. He crosses the room in three strides and scoops Mom up in his big arms.

"Are you ready for vacation?"

"Yes." Mom giggles as he sets her down.

Like always, I'm struck by how much younger and carefree she seems whenever Jean-Marc is around. She's dated other people here and there since my dad died, but she's been with Jean-Marc the longest.

Jean-Marc turns his attention to me, and as he walks closer, I realize that his T-shirt is decorated with small coconut trees.

"Someone's feeling festive," I say.

"Don't be jealous." He plops down on the edge of the bed next to me, and it creaks under his weight. Jean-Marc is huge. Almost three times my size. I'm not even kidding. He was a bodybuilder when he lived in Haiti, but he stopped once he moved here. Like Mom, he's an emergency room nurse, and he's one of the gentlest people I've ever met. He's the type of person who gets excited when he enters contests to win a brand-new sports car or vacations to Tahiti. He's probably entered, and lost, thousands of contests. It's like a hobby. But that changed a couple weeks ago when he won two free tickets to a cruise in the Caribbean. Part of me thinks this is the only reason Mom decided to go.

Right now, she's pacing around the room, muttering to herself. She pauses and bites her lip, something she does when she's nervous. Jean-Marc sighs and walks over to zip up her suitcase. "Carol, we need to go. If we don't leave now, we'll miss our flight. The meter is running."

And I'll be late to my audition because I can't leave until you're gone.

"Okay," Mom says. She grabs her Bible from her bedside table and drops it inside her suitcase.

Jean-Marc reaches for the suitcase, but Mom swats his hand away. "Just let me check one more time to make sure I have everything."

He reaches again, and this time he grabs it and lifts the suitcase high out of her reach.

"No, no, no," he says. "I'm not spending all of my vacation money on the taxi before he's even taken us to the airport. We have to actually make it to Florida in order to get on the cruise ship."

He leaves the room, and seconds later, his big feet pound down the stairs. Mom stares at her doorway, then looks at me. Her lips slowly shift into a frown.

"I don't know about this, baby," she says.

My stomach drops. "Know about what?"

"I can't leave you here alone. I'm not comfortable with it." She rubs a hand over her face and looks around her room.

"Maybe we can wait until summer, when I have enough money to bring you with us." She stares at a spot on the wall, still frowning. "Yes, that's what I'll do. This is silly, leaving you here for a week."

"No!" I jump up, and Mom startles. "You have to go. When's the last time you went on vacation?"

She waves me off. "I can always plan another vacation."

She heads for the stairs. I have to do something to stop her, to change her mind.

I grab her shoulders and turn her to face me. "If you don't go, I'll blame myself. Jean-Marc is so excited about this trip. You know he's never won anything before. If you don't go, you'll break his heart, and I'll have to live with the fact that it was because of me."

She blinks. I'm definitely laying the dramatics on thick right now, but I have to do what I have to do.

"I'll be fine," I continue. "I've stayed at Reina's plenty of times. Her parents will take care of me. Mrs. Acosta said so herself."

Mom sighs. "I know, but I'll still be worried about you. I know how you get with your nightmares. I don't want you to have dreams about something bad happening to me every night."

I hug her so she'll stop talking, and I feel her tense shoulders relax.

When I pull away, she looks at me closely. People always comment on how similar we look. We're the same height and have the same brown eyes and medium-brown complexion. But I know that when she looks at me, she sees traces of my dad. I wonder what it must feel like to see the person you've lost and the person you could lose all at once. I lay my head on her shoulder so she can't see the guilt on my face.

"I'll be fine," I repeat.

Jean-Marc calls for her again. We break apart, and I follow her outside. Jean-Marc and the taxi driver are piling their suitcases into the trunk. The taxi driver says something to Jean-Marc in Creole, and they burst into laughter.

Mom abruptly freezes and sprints back toward the house, yelling that she forgot her makeup bag. Jean-Marc groans, and he and the taxi driver continue their conversation.

There's a sudden commotion at the house directly across the street. I watch as the screen door swings open, and Geezer, my neighbor's pit bull, gallops down the porch steps as fast as his old legs will allow. Then Eli Greene, AKA the worst person on the planet, steps outside, and he looks up and down the street. He pauses when his eyes land on me. I suck in a breath and wait for him to turn away like he usually does, but he lifts his hand . . . and waves.

Is he waving at *me*?

Not possible. We haven't spoken in over a year. I glance at Jean-Marc and the taxi driver. Neither is looking in Eli's direction. When I look back at Eli—as if I didn't see him the first time—he waves *again*.

Okay. This is weird. And suspicious. I'm so stunned that

without thinking, I actually lift my hand and wave back. Oh my God. Why did I just do that? I shouldn't be waving at Eli! He's public enemy number one and I don't want him thinking otherwise.

The sun is in my eyes, so I'm not exactly sure if this is true, but it looks like Eli is smiling. *Smiling.* What is happening? And why am I just becoming conscious of the fact that I stepped outside in my pink heart-print pajamas, still wearing a hair bonnet?

Flustered, I spin around and collide with Mom. She tosses her makeup bag into the back seat of the taxi.

"I'll try to find a way to call you from the cruise ship," she says, but we both know she probably won't be able to. Apparently, getting Wi-Fi on cruises is really expensive, and Mom and Jean-Marc don't plan on spending any unnecessary money during this free vacation.

She stands there, uncertainty clouding her features. For a moment, I'm afraid she's going to try to cancel the trip again. "And if anything goes wrong at the Acostas', Ms. Linda doesn't mind if you stay with her. Our flight lands Sunday evening, so we'll be back in time for Easter dinner."

She goes through all the emergency and safety protocols. If Ms. Linda doesn't answer, I should call her coworker, Eileen. Watch my surroundings. Always carry a little bit of cash, don't just rely on my debit card. If someone tries to rob me, throw my purse and run. I've heard this speech so many times I can recite it word for word.

"Don't throw any wild parties while we're gone," Jean-Marc says, winking, giving me a hug good-bye.

I smile. "I promise I won't. You guys go ahead. You'll miss your flight."

"Please take care of yourself," Mom says.

She hugs me again and climbs into the back seat. Jean-Marc slides in next to her. They lean out of the window and wave as they drive away. Mom still looks worried. I wave back until they turn the corner and I can't see them anymore.

Against my better judgment, I glance across the street. Eli is still there, pacing back and forth with his phone pressed to his ear.

I don't have time to wonder why he smiled at me. Or to wonder about him at all. I turn around and race back into the house. D.C. is three hours away, and I have to be there by two p.m. It's only ten a.m. now, but I hate the highway—and driving, in general—so I want to give myself extra time.

I tear up the stairs to my room and drag the duffel bag with all my dance gear from underneath my bed. I throw off my pajamas and slide on my pink tights and my new purple leotard. I put on my scuffed purple high-top Chucks to match. I quickly take off my bonnet and brush my hair into a topknot.

Before I leave my room, I stand on my bed and jump up to kiss my Avery Johnson poster for good luck. Then I go to my dresser and kiss my favorite photo of my dad standing in front of our house, cradling baby me in his arms. He's smiling at Mom, who's holding the camera. Mom always says that he was a good dancer, and that's where I get it from. She also says that he was clumsy, but I didn't get that gene. Sometimes I envy that she has so many memories of him when I don't have any. I'd like to think that if he were here, he'd give me a kiss for good luck, too.

I run downstairs, but when I grab the doorknob, I pause. Is it really worth going to D.C. and lying to Mom?

I imagine myself at the audition, in a room full of dancers who didn't spend seven months out of the studio to have surgery and then rehabilitate. Dancers who, unlike me, are in top-notch form. But then I imagine myself a year and a half from now, sitting in a college classroom, learning about things that have nothing at all to do with ballet. The kind of life I don't want.

With a new surge of energy, I open my front door and smack right into the person standing on the other side.

Chapter 2

A Favor for a Favor

"What's up, Chloe?"

I don't mean to shriek, but I do it anyway. I clamp my hand over my mouth and stumble backward. Eli Greene is standing there with his fist raised, ready to knock. He grins at me, and I think about the Big Bad Wolf when he came for the Three Little Pigs.

"Sorry!" Eli says, holding up his hands in apology. "I didn't mean to scare you."

I stare at him, willing my pulse to return to normal. It's just Eli. Not a killer. Not someone coming to abduct me. Not Mom or Jean-Marc returning for another forgotten item, about to catch me in the act.

"Shit," Eli says. "That scream was *loud*."

He grins from ear to ear, flashing his white teeth. I think of the Big Bad Wolf again. Eli always smiles like he knows something that you don't. With that smile and his light-brown complexion, he looks like the lead singer of an R & B group. Except I know he can't sing . . . or dance.

"What do you want?" I finally ask.

I step outside and lock the door behind me. Eli only moves back a few inches, so when I turn around, he's right there. I get a whiff of cigarette smoke and fresh laundry. He keeps getting taller. Right now, he towers over me. It's hard to believe we were once the same height.

He's wearing his usual getup: a T-shirt, basketball shorts, and Timberland boots. Today everything is black, aside from his bright blue Phillies baseball cap. He's a modern-day grim reaper.

"Where are you going?" he asks. His eyes shift to the duffel bag slung over my shoulder.

"I—" *Play it cool, Chloe.* "Nowhere. Mind your business."

The corner of his mouth twitches. "You're hiding something."

"No, I'm not." I push past him and walk toward my car, but he falls into step right beside me. His boots clomp annoyingly with each step. "Go away."

"Let me guess," he says. "You're running away. But the question is, *to where*? The circus? To be with some old dude your mom doesn't approve of? Nah, that's not like you." We reach my car and he leans against the driver's-side door, blocking me from grabbing the handle. "Ah, I know. You're going to a convent. That's a great choice. You'd make an amazing nun."

I glare at him. He laughs.

"Move." I try to push him out of the way, but he doesn't budge.

"Where are you going? I promise I won't tell."

"Why do you want to know so badly?"

He shrugs. "You never go anywhere or do anything, so I'm intrigued."

"I do things all the time. I just don't tell *you* about them." *Relax. He's trying to bait you. Stick to the plan.* "I'm going to Reina's house, okay? That's it. Nothing special. Now go away."

"Interesting," Eli says. "Isn't Reina working at some camp over spring break?"

"What?" HOW COULD HE POSSIBLY KNOW THAT? "How . . ."

"I heard Reina talking about it at school. You know she's loud as hell." His ear-to-ear grin returns. "So you must really be running away if you had to lie. You know, when they report that you're missing, they're going to interview me because I'll be the last person who saw you before you left. They might even show the interview on *20/20*. You should watch if you have access to a TV in the convent."

"I'M NOT RUNNING AWAY."

So much for keeping my cool. But I don't care. I won't tell him anything. His mom, Ms. Linda, is Mom's best friend. And the last thing I need to do is slip up and tell him where

I'm really going so that he can tell Ms. Linda, and Ms. Linda will call Mom, and then Mom will call me, and she will be on the first flight back to New Jersey, and all my plans will be ruined. I'll never get to audition. I'll never be a professional ballerina. I'll never—

"Hey, did you hear me?" Eli snaps his fingers in my face.

"Don't do that. It's rude," I grumble, pushing his hand away. "What do you *want*?"

"I just told you. I need a favor."

The last time Eli asked me for a favor, I was eleven and he was twelve. He told me he dropped his house keys in the thornbush in front of his porch, and he asked me to grab them because my arms were skinnier. To prove I wasn't afraid, I dove my arm into the thornbush just for Eli to tell me he'd never actually dropped his keys. He was only joking, and he didn't really think I'd be brave enough to do it.

I glance down at the thin scar that trails up my right forearm. Eli follows my gaze. I know he remembers, because he looks at my arm and winces.

"Come on," he says. "That happened when we were kids."

"I have to go." I throw my duffel bag in my back seat and reach for the driver's-side door.

"Wait," he says, pressing his palm against the handle.

I sigh, frustrated. "How many times do I have to tell you to go away?"

"Listen, I know you hate me, but—"

"Is that what you think? That I hate you?"

He blinks. "Well . . . yeah."

"I don't hate you," I say, because it's true. *Hate* is a strong word that shouldn't be used lightly. Do I dislike him? Yes.

Eli looks hopeful.

"But that doesn't mean I want to help you. Even if I did, I can't," I say. "I'm already running late."

"Cool. Whatever." He turns on his heel and stomps down the driveway. He looks silly. Like a six-foot-tall child who is angry that he couldn't get his way. "When my mom gets home, I'll tell her you were packing up your car and refused to tell me where you were going. She'll call the cops in two seconds."

My stomach drops, but I try to hide my panic. "It doesn't matter if you tell your mom, because my mom already knows where I'm going!" I call to him as he walks away, but he just glances over his shoulder and shrugs.

"If that's true, then it won't be a big deal when my mom finds out."

When he's almost across the street, my panic gets the best of me.

"Fine!" I shout. "I'm going to a dance audition, okay?"

He turns around and raises an eyebrow. He slowly makes his way back across the street, and my blood boils as I watch him take each step.

"Where at?" he asks once he's in front of me.

"Don't worry about it. Just know I'm going to an audition and I'm coming right home afterward."

"I'm afraid that's not enough information. I'm still going to have to tell my mom just in case something bad happens to you."

"The audition is in D.C.," I hear myself snap.

Slowly, his whole face lights up. "D.C.? For real?"

No, no, no. WHY DID I JUST TELL HIM WHERE I'M GOING?

I try to keep my voice calm. "Yeah, so don't tell your mom."

"This is perfect," he says. "I have to go to North Carolina to see my dad this week, and I was gonna ask you to give me a ride to the train station, but I can catch the train from D.C. and cut the trip in half."

"Wait . . . what?"

"You can drop me off at the train station on the way to your audition thing."

"No." My mind is reeling. "No. No. No."

"No?" He looks genuinely surprised.

"No! Why can't you drive yourself?"

He gestures across the street to his empty driveway. "My mom's car is in the shop, so she borrowed mine."

"No." It's fascinating how my vocabulary has been reduced to one word.

"Come on," he says, clasping his hands together in prayer. "Do this solid for me. I hate the train ride from Jersey to North Carolina. I'll be stuck on that shit all day."

"Why can't you call your mom and ask her to take you?"

He glances back at his house and scowls. "I did call her, but she's not answering. She was supposed to be back in the morning to drop me off at the station, but she's still out with her new boyfriend, I guess."

"Oh."

Great. Now I feel bad for him.

"Come on." He turns to face me again. A grin replaces his scowl. "If you take me, I promise not to tell my mom where you're going." When I start to speak, he holds up his hand. "And I know your mom has no idea what you plan to do because there's no way she'd let you drive to D.C. by yourself."

I shake my head. "I seriously can't believe you're blackmailing me right now."

"'Blackmail' is a bit much, don't you think? Think of it more like, 'I won't scratch your back if you don't scratch mine.'"

He smiles. I guess his intent is to charm me. Girls at school swoon over him and his clichéd bad-boy mojo whatever-you-call-it. Eli is handsome and he can be charismatic when he wants. I've always known this about him. But what a lot of people don't know is that Eli might be nice to look at, but underneath he's rough and calloused. Like a pair of battered feet hidden inside pretty pointe shoes.

I don't want to drive anywhere with him. *Walking* to D.C. would actually be preferable. And it's already stressful enough to drive on the highway by myself. Having him there would only make things worse.

But I can't risk him telling his mom. If he does, everything will be over for me.

I can't believe he's stooping this low.

And I *really* can't believe I'm about to say this.

I gulp. "Fine . . . I'll give you a ride."

"Cool." Eli grins and claps his hands together. "Just let me grab my bag, and Geezer, and—"

"*Geezer?*" At the sound of his name, Geezer sits up on Eli's porch and perks his ears. "No way."

Eli pauses. "What's the problem?"

"Geezer can't get in my car! He stinks and he'll get hair all over my back seat. And I don't even think he likes me." He barks at me whenever I walk by their house, which is proof enough.

Eli narrows his eyes. "Geezer does *not* stink. I bathe him weekly."

"No." I shake my head. "And how are you going to put him on the train with you, anyway? That's probably not allowed."

He doesn't look fazed. "Don't worry about it."

How did my morning come to this? I'm being punished for lying to my mom. It's the only explanation.

"He's old, Chloe," Eli says. "I just want to take him to the beach by my dad's house so he can run in the sand one last time before he dies."

I roll my eyes. "He's not *that* old."

"I won't speak a word to my mom if you take me *and*

Chapter 3

Road Trip

I try to approach driving the same way that I approach ballet. With precision, grace, and absolute concentration. At ballet, I succeed. At driving, I fail. Miserably. I don't feel comfortable behind the wheel. The reasons are obvious: my dad died in a car accident, and I almost got hit by a car.

"Why are you driving so slow?" Eli asks. "The speed limit is sixty-five."

I'm driving in the slow lane and only doing 50 miles per hour. To be fair, if I drive too fast, my car starts to shake. It's a 2005 Honda Civic: not ancient, but old enough. I don't want to push it too hard, but I speed up to 60 miles per hour when I realize every car is going around me. One lady gives me the stink eye as she passes. I want to be mad, but I can only admire her ability to give the stink eye, accelerate, *and* switch lanes at the same time.

"Sorry," I mumble, even though I know she can't hear me.

Out of the corner of my eye, I can see Eli bouncing his

knee and tapping his fingers against his thighs. He is, and always has been, someone who fidgets. He reaches up and touches the ballet-shoe key chain that hangs behind my rearview mirror. Then he turns around and scratches Geezer's head.

"You know, his name used to be Albert," he says to me. "That's what they called him at the shelter."

I ignore him. My intention is to speak to him as little as possible. The moment I drop him off at the train station will be the most relieving moment of my life.

"I thought Albert was a dumbass name for a dog," he continues. "So I changed it to Geezer, since he's so old."

What if Geezer actually preferred being called Albert? It's sad that pets never get a say in anything that happens to them. I'm not a pet, but that's how I feel sometimes when it comes to Mom.

"This silence is killing me," Eli says. He fiddles with the radio, but gets frustrated when every station is playing commercials.

If driving on the highway weren't so stressful, I'd have yelled at him for touching my radio without permission. But I'm hoping that some music will help me relax. I make playlists for everything: dancing, cleaning, when I'm deep-conditioning my hair. A few months ago, Jean-Marc installed a new radio in my car so that I could hook up my phone and play music. I've been so thrown off by Eli's presence that I forgot about the playlist I made for the drive. It has all my favorites. Beyoncé, SZA, Drake, and some Jhené Aiko, too.

"I have an aux cord in my glove compartment," I tell him. "Hook my phone up to it and choose the playlist called *D.C.*"

Eli follows my directions, and "Drew Barrymore" by SZA begins to play. I feel calmer once I hear her voice. I'm even doing a good job at humming and focusing on the road at the same time. If only Reina could see me now. I always make her drive. All the merging and guardrails and other cars make me so nervous, but right now I feel fine!

"What *is* this?" Eli says.

I glance at him. His eyes are widened in horror.

"What is what?" I say, confused.

"This song." He holds his hands over his ears. "It's making my ears bleed."

"What are you talking about? This is a great song."

He snorts. "You and I have different ideas of the word *great*." Without asking, he unplugs my phone and plugs in his instead.

"What are you doing?" I say. "You can't go around touching my stuff! You're a guest in this car!"

He waves me off. "I'm enlightening you." He turns the volume knob all the way up. Then a beat blares so loudly through the speakers that I feel the bass vibrate throughout my entire body. Geezer wakes up and starts to bark, and I swerve a little into the lane beside me. A passing driver beeps his horn and shakes his fist. My heart feels like it's in my throat.

"THE WU-TANG CLAN," Eli shouts above the music. "THIS IS WHAT YOU CALL GREAT."

I want to throttle him.

Instead, I channel my anger into yanking out the aux cord and throwing his phone into his lap.

Very slowly, he says, "I can't believe you just did that." He slides his phone into his pocket. "Have it your way."

I try to ignore him and stay focused on the road, but I'm distracted again when I hear the sound of a lighter being flicked. It doesn't register that Eli is actually smoking until he's already taken a puff and the smell of tobacco fills the car. I find myself shrieking for the second time today.

"YOU CAN'T SMOKE IN HERE."

"Sheesh." He flicks his cigarette out of the window without any regard to the other cars on the highway. "Sorry. Chill out."

Chill out?!

I roll each window completely down to get rid of the tobacco smell. I'm so mad that I'm gripping the steering wheel with all my might. There's a chance I'll kill him before we make it out of New Jersey.

"You still do that weird thing with your nose when you get mad," he says.

"What weird thing?" I cover my nose with my hand, suddenly self-conscious. "What weird nose thing?"

He twitches his nose like a rabbit. "Like that."

"And you still . . . you still . . ." I'm trying to think of a snarky comeback. Eli waits, looking amused. "You still have crooked teeth on the bottom row." The minute I say it, I regret it. Weak. So weak. I could have done better than that.

"Wow, Chlo. That really hurt my feelings." I don't have to look at him to know that he's grinning.

"I don't want you to talk to me for the rest of the drive," I snap. "Just be quiet."

"Fine with me." He turns his attention to his phone and doesn't say anything else.

Eli's always had a way of getting under my skin. Like at my eighth birthday party when he kept threatening to stick his hand in my cake before we sang "Happy Birthday." Or my first day of freshman year when he tricked me into believing that underclassmen had a separate cafeteria and I spent all of my lunch period looking for it. And then, of course, there was the fight we had last year before Homecoming. Each time always resulted in me screaming at him like a maniac, and each time I felt stupid afterward for letting him make me so upset.

The most we ever got along was during middle school when our friend Trey Mason lived around the corner. Too sweet and unwilling to argue about whether we'd ride bikes or go to the community pool, Trey was great at steering us toward a middle ground. Then he moved to Delaware the summer before he and Eli started high school. I haven't seen him since.

People are driving a lot faster once I merge onto the

turnpike. I can hear the wind as they fly past me in the slow lane. A guy zips by on a motorcycle and my stomach clenches.

How do people drive on this every day?

"So what's up with not telling your mom about this trip?" Eli asks.

I give him a look to remind him that he shouldn't be talking to me, but I'm sure it's less intimidating than I mean for it to be. You can't look threatening while also looking freaked out about driving.

"What?" He throws his arms up. "You won't let me play any music. The least you can do is talk to me." He sighs when I don't answer. "I'm sorry about smoking in your car, okay?"

I wait. Is that all he's sorry about?

It must be, because he doesn't say anything else.

"My audition is for a dance conservatory in New York City. She doesn't want me to live there."

"Why not?"

"Probably because she doesn't think it's safe."

I don't have to explain much else. Eli knows how Mom is. When he was twelve, she discovered him trying to climb the cherry tree in our backyard. He was so startled when she caught him, he almost lost his grip on the bark and fell. Then she lectured him for an hour on the different bones he could have broken and how long they would've taken to heal.

Eli asks where she and Jean-Marc were going this morning, and I tell him about the free cruise tickets. Before he can ask another Mom-related question, I remind him that I made a no-talking rule.

He's quiet for all of four seconds before he says, "Larissa's coming home for Easter this year."

"Really?" I break my own rule, because this intrigues me. Ms. Linda invited Mom and me to Easter dinner, too, but I had no idea Larissa would be there. I haven't seen Eli's older sister in years. We text every now and then, but she goes to college all the way in Virginia and she never comes home. She spends her summers doing internships near her college and she's at their dad's house during the holidays. When I was younger, I wanted to be just like her. It's funny how once people are out of sight, they become out of mind, too.

"Yeah. My mom threw a fit and said Riss never comes home to see her. Blah, blah. She guilt-tripped her." He shrugs. "After my dad forces me to tour UNC on Saturday, I'm gonna catch the train home so I can see her."

"Oh, right," I say, remembering Ms. Linda told Mom and me that Eli will be a freshman at the University of North Carolina in the fall. "Pre-law, right?"

He shrugs again. "Maybe, maybe not."

"What are your other options?"

With a sigh, he says, "I'm still pissed my parents didn't take my clown school dreams seriously."

I roll my eyes. I will gladly go back to ignoring him now.

But then Geezer sits up in the back seat and starts pacing. He whines when he realizes he has no way out of the car.

"What's wrong with him?" I ask. His restlessness makes me nervous.

Eli turns around and rubs Geezer's head. His deep voice turns soft. "What's wrong, boy? You okay?" To me, he says, "He has a weak bladder. He probably needs to pee."

In the distance, I see an exit for a rest stop. We're not even out of New Jersey and I already have to pull over.

"No, this will put me behind schedule," I argue.

"It's either that or he goes all over your back seat," Eli says. *Why* did I let him and his dog come with me? I can't believe I was stupid enough to fall for his blackmailing trick.

Quickly—or as quickly as a driver like me can go—I take the rest stop exit and pray that Geezer can keep it together until he's out of my car. When I pull into a parking spot, I turn to Eli and he's already looking at me.

"There you go again with the nose twitching," he says.

❦

Eli and Geezer take off toward the woods by the picnic area. I check my phone and see that I have two texts. One is from Ms. Linda asking if I've seen Eli. I'm not going to answer her. There's no way I'm lying to someone else's mom, too. Eli will have to deal with that on his own.

The other text is from Reina, sent two minutes ago. It's a picture of a soggy-looking sandwich and a small bag of potato chips.

This is what they're feeding us at camp. Save me ☹

I FaceTime her and pray that she's still on a lunch break.

"Hello!" she sings when she answers. She's sitting on a bench, wearing a bright orange T-shirt that says CAMP CENTER STAGE and her favorite cat-eye sunglasses that make her look like a movie star. Her dark curls are piled into a bun. "How is my professional-ballerina-to-be? Are you in D.C. yet?"

"No." A few yards away I can see Eli and Geezer standing in between two trees. Eli leans against a tree and lights a cigarette. So gross.

Reina lifts her sunglasses and brings the phone closer to her face. "You look absolutely miserable, Chlo. What's wrong?"

"You will not believe who I'm with right now."

"Wait . . . this isn't an SOS call, is it? Is a creep lurking around, trying to kidnap you?"

"What? No!" Sometimes her level of dramatics still surprises me. "I'm with Eli Greene."

She blinks and shakes her head. "I'm sorry. Do you mean Eli Greene . . . as in neighbor-who-we-no-longer-speak-to-under-any-circumstances Eli Greene?"

"Yes," I say. "That one."

"*What?* How in the world did that happen?"

"I don't know," I groan, sliding a hand over my face. I tell her how he threatened to blackmail me.

Reina sucks her teeth. "What an asshole."

"I know." I watch as Eli and Geezer make their way back toward me. Geezer trots happily now that his bladder is empty, and Eli swings his lanky arms like he has not a care in the world. Like being around me doesn't make him feel awkward or sorry for what he's done in the past.

I swallow thickly. "I'm starting to get nauseous. I think feeling nervous about my audition, and the stress of him being here is getting to me."

"I can't believe you used to have a crush on him," she says, rolling her eyes.

"Can we *please* pretend that never happened?"

"I am more than happy to do that." She lowers her voice. "Did he bring up . . . ?"

"No," I say quickly. "And I doubt he ever will."

Eli is closer now. Close enough to hear what I'm saying. "I have to go," I tell Reina. "I'm about to start driving again."

"Call me when you get to D.C.," she says. "And listen, don't be afraid to kick him out of your car and leave him on the side of the highway. You're being nicer to him than you should be."

"I'll keep that in mind," I say. Though we both know I would never do something like that.

I hang up as Eli approaches. I tell him that his mom texted, and he sighs.

"I'll call her," he says. He lets Geezer in the back seat and sticks his head in the passenger-side window, peering at me. "Are you okay? Your face looks weird."

I roll my eyes. "Wow, thanks."

"I'm serious. You look like you're about to throw up."

"I'm fine," I say, annoyed. "Hurry up and get in the car. I have an audition to get to, in case you forgot."

"I'm just gonna grab some stuff from the convenience store really quick." When I groan, he says, "Relax. It'll take two seconds."

He walks away and Geezer whines, clearly unhappy to be left with me. I wait for him to stop, but he doesn't. I'll never understand the bond dogs have with their owners. Mom never let me have a dog. She read an article once about a Rottweiler that bit a toddler in the face, and that was that.

When Eli comes back outside, he's carrying a plastic bag full of snacks. He sits in the passenger seat and pulls out a pack of Starbursts. When he was younger, he used to take the wrappers and fold them into different shapes: cranes, cubes, stars.

I'm surprised when he tosses a bottle of ginger ale into my lap.

"For your stomach," he says.

He looks a little unsure, like he's afraid I might throw the bottle back in his face. For the first time today, I think that maybe Eli wants to tell me he's sorry, but he doesn't know how.

"Thank you," I say.

"You're welcome." He clears his throat. "So, listen. Why don't you let me drive the rest of the way? We'll get there faster."

I almost choke on my sip of soda. "Absolutely not."

"You want to be rid of us, don't you?" he says. "If I drive, we'll be in D.C. and out of your car in no time. Plus, you don't have to worry about driving with a messed-up stomach."

The last time I depended on Eli to drive me somewhere, things ended badly. I don't trust him. But I *do* want to be rid of them, he does drive faster, and I want my nausea to go away. If letting him drive means that I won't be late to my audition, then I guess I can stand him sitting behind my wheel for the next two hours.

Hesitantly, I open my door so we can switch seats, but I pause before getting out all the way.

"You can't play your music," I warn.

He flashes his wolfish grin. "I didn't expect to."

When we pass each other in front of the car, I find myself agreeing with Reina. I can't believe I used to have a crush on him, either.

Chapter 4

The World's Smallest Circus

As we drive over the Delaware Memorial Bridge, I look down at the greenish, murky water below us and realize my nausea is getting worse. The ridiculous decision I've made to go to this audition is finally starting to sink in. I don't know if I'm ready.

I can't stop thinking about the night I broke my ankle right before the Homecoming dance last year. While walking to the school in heels, I ran to get out of the way of a car that was trying to run a red light, and I lost my footing and tripped once I reached the curb. My ankle bent as I fell, and I heard the crack before I actually felt any pain. But then I did feel the pain, and it was excruciating. Later, at the hospital, they told me that my ankle was fractured. A fractured ankle meant no ballet. It meant I would no longer be the Snow Queen in our upcoming production of *The Nutcracker*. It meant all my hard work was going right down the drain.

I spent seven months rehabilitating and watching the other dancers in my studio get cast for roles that should have been mine, and nine more months of playing catch-up. I'll be the first to admit that I've never been the most confident person *offstage*. I don't raise my hand to answer questions in class or easily strike up conversations with strangers. In everyday life, I fold into myself and blend in with the crowd a little too well. But when it came to ballet, I always stood out. I moved with grace and strength. Since my injury, though, I spend so much time second-guessing myself, nervous that I'm not dancing as well as I used to, or that if I do something wrong I'll get hurt all over again. The uncertainty shows.

After my surgery, my doctor told me that I'd never be the dancer I once was. That haunts me. What if he's right? What if I go to this audition and completely embarrass myself?

What in the world was I thinking?

Eli smoothly weaves in and out of traffic. He's getting us to D.C. much faster than I would have, but the weaving rhythm makes my stomach churn.

"You really need more practice driving on the highway," he says. He switches into the middle lane to get around a bus and easily merges back into the fast lane. Other cars whiz past us, and I close my eyes to keep from feeling dizzy. "I know that everyone can't be as good a driver as me, but you can be *almost* as good if you try. When's the last time you even drove on the highway before today?"

I shrug and stay quiet. I can feel the bile at the top of my throat, threatening to rush out at any moment.

"When my dad gave me my Camaro last year, I drove

straight to the highway," he says. "Camaros aren't meant for suburban roads. They're too fast. On the way home, I picked up Isiah. He was jealous as hell."

I peek one eye open and glance at him at the mention of Isiah's name. Isiah Brown is Eli's idiotic best friend, who is mostly known for making stupid jokes, sleeping in class, and hitting on girls who have zero interest in him. Isiah used to tease Eli and Trey endlessly when we were younger, but somehow, he and Eli became friends after Eli quit the basketball team. Eli was already popular for being a good basketball player, but his popularity skyrocketed when he became friends with Isiah, the class clown. Last Halloween, they dressed as Kris Kross and won first place in the costume contest. They didn't even do anything but hop around the stage, barely mouthing the lyrics to "jump," but they still got more votes than Reina, who did an amazing rendition of Lady Macbeth's soliloquy.

"I don't know why I let my mom borrow my car," he continues. "She always tells me I'm inconsiderate, and the moment I do something nice for her, *she's* inconsiderate."

I swallow and ignore the terrible taste, daring to open my mouth. "Eli—"

"Her boyfriend, or whatever guy she went out with, should have picked her up. Why the hell did she have to borrow my car to go see him?"

I squeeze my eyes closed again. *You're fine, Chloe. You don't need to stress out. So what if you fail? It won't be the end of the world. At least Avery Johnson will finally know you exist.*

I'm only making things worse. I grip the sides of the seat to hold myself in place. "Eli—"

"You know why he didn't pick her up? Because he's a bum. That's all she dates these days. Bums."

I turn to face him. "ELI."

"What?"

When he finally gives me his attention, it's too late. I'm already puking all over the front of my new leotard . . . and I get some on his arm.

"YOOOOO." His eyes grow as wide as golf balls.

He shoves the plastic bag that once held his snacks into my lap while cutting across the highway in a frantic attempt to pull over. Angry drivers honk at us, and the ruckus combined with Eli's breakneck speed wakes Geezer from his nap, and he starts barking again. I wonder what a sight we must be: Eli shouting *FUCK* and *HOLY SHIT* and *WHAT THE HELL, CHLOE,* over and over; Geezer running from window to window as if he's rabid; and me, vomiting into a plastic bag. We're the world's smallest circus.

Eli grips the steering wheel with new ferocity and presses on the brake as we merge into the slow lane. For one second he takes his eyes off the road to look at me. His gaze is hard and concerned. Then his expression turns grim as he glances at the throwup covering his arm.

We both turn our attention back to the road at the same

time. I notice that the old silver Impala in front of us has a license plate that reads HIP PIE before it comes to an abrupt stop and Eli slams into the back of it.

There's the loud *bang* of metal crashing against metal. Geezer goes nuts and starts barking at an all-time high. I wish everything would slow down so I can process what's happening. A minute ago, we were in motion, and now we aren't.

I see smoke rising from the hood of my car. I touch my face, my neck, my arms, my legs. Nothing is broken. I think of my dad, and how lucky I am to be alive.

"Fuck, fuck, fuck." Eli's voice is low and panicked. He twists around to check on Geezer, who is curled up in a ball in the back seat, unharmed. Eli turns back around, presses his face into the steering wheel, and grips his head with his hands. Slowly, he leans back and looks at me. "I'm sorry, Chloe. *Fuck*."

Then he lowers his hands from his head and I suck in a breath.

"What?" he says, running his hands over his face, checking for scars or bruises.

"You have a bald spot," I say, and it's ridiculous because we just got into an accident and my car could be totaled, but this is the only thing I can clearly focus on. Right in the middle of Eli's thick, dark curls is a big bald spot the shape of a jagged square. "Why do you have a *bald spot*?"

"Who gives a shit?!" He reaches up to cover his head, brushing his fingers over the exposed patch of skin. "I just crashed your car!"

The woman who drove the Impala is standing by the guardrail, surveying the accident with a perplexed expression. She's really tall and skinny. Like a human ostrich, with pale skin and long blond hair. She's wearing a flowy orange dress and worn sandals. I realize her license plate isn't referencing a weird type of pie, but that it says *hippie*. Oddly enough, her car hasn't been harmed at all. Just a tiny dent in her back bumper. She walks over to my window and leans down so that her face is level with mine. She has to hold her wavy hair back with her hands. This close I can see that she's youngish, probably in her early twenties.

"Are you guys all right?" she asks. Her voice is so soft, I have to lean forward to hear her. Her eyes shift from my face to the throwup on my leotard, and I reach for the napkins in my glove compartment in a hurried attempt to clean myself up. I hand some napkins to Eli so he can wipe off his arm.

"We're okay," I say. Although my shaky voice would indicate otherwise.

"You might want to get out and look at the damage," she says. "We'll have to call the police and report this."

My stomach sinks way down into my feet, out of my shoes, and goes running down the highway. *The police?*

Eli groans and mumbles something under his breath. The woman glances at him, and I wish for once he would just be quiet. We both open our doors, and I see how much traffic has gathered. People are driving by slowly to be nosy.

Eli makes sure Geezer is secure in the back seat and we

follow her to the front of my car. When I see the damage, I feel like I might be sick again.

My headlights are completely smashed and glass litters the ground. There's a huge dent in the front bumper, like it ran into the Incredible Hulk's fist. Everything looks sad and broken and hopeless. Exactly how I feel inside. Because now I know that there is absolutely no way I will make it to the audition.

And—oh my God. *Mom.* She's going to kill me when she sees what's happened!

Eli takes a step closer to the car and bends down, tapping his knuckles against the destroyed bumper. He winces and then turns around to look at me. "It's not so bad."

"WHAT?" In seconds I'm standing right above him, pointing my finger inches from his nose. "What do you mean it's not so bad? This is TERRIBLE, and it's your fault! You're not in a Fast & Furious movie. News flash: my Honda is not your Camaro!"

"*My* fault?" He stands up straight, reminding me who the bigger person actually is. His nostrils flare. "*You're* the one who threw up all over me! I was trying to pull over!"

The Impala woman stands in between us before I can say anything else. "Arguing isn't going to solve anything," she says. Eli and I immediately stop talking. Maybe it's because of her peaceful hippie aura. "Can you tell me whose car this is?"

"Hers," Eli says at the same time that I say, "Mine."

"I'm Natalie," she says to me. "Do you have your

insurance and registration so that we can exchange information? We should take care of that before we contact the police."

"I'm Chloe. And yes, I have it." I bite my lip and hold back tears. Mom's insurance will skyrocket after we report this accident. She'll never trust me with anything again.

I start to walk to my car to get my information, but Eli grabs on to my arm, stopping me.

"Wait a second," he whispers. "Let me try to handle this first."

"What are you talking about?" I whisper back, glancing at Natalie. Her perplexed expression has returned.

"Just listen to me for once."

He rolls his shoulders back and flashes a smile as if he's getting ready to deliver a speech. I don't understand why he's doing this until he turns around and flashes this smile at Natalie. Right away, she blushes.

"I'm Eli," he says, gently taking her hand in his. "It's very nice to meet you, Natalie. I'm sorry it had to happen under these circumstances." His smile grows, dimples deepen. Natalie smiles back shyly. It doesn't surprise me that he has the same effect on her that he does on girls our age. "Natalie, you seem like an understanding person. Do you think it's really necessary to get insurance companies involved? There's barely any damage to your car."

Natalie glances at the small dent in her bumper. "This

car is a tank. A '72 Impala. My grandfather gave it to me when I graduated from college."

"Nice," Eli says. "It's a beauty."

Natalie nods in agreement, but she still doesn't look completely convinced. If Eli notices this, too, he doesn't let on.

"Hey, can you check on Geezer?" he asks me.

"Huh?" I turn around and look at Geezer. He's poking his head out of the back-seat window, watching cars drive by. "He's fine."

"He might need water." Eli's eyebrows are doing something funky. It takes me a second to realize he's giving me a look that says he has a plan. And me standing here is not helping said plan. "I packed his water bowl in my bag."

"Okay," I say, walking away.

Geezer looks at me suspiciously as I open the back-seat door, but he starts to wag his tail when he sees me pull his water bowl from Eli's bag. I place it flat on the back seat, and Geezer is already shoving his long tongue into the bowl before I've even poured all the water out of my water bottle.

I can't hear what Eli is saying to Natalie, but I can see that he's making her laugh. She glances at me in the car and frowns a little. What is he telling her?

Whatever he's saying must be working. As he talks, Natalie nods her head like she's hypnotized. Then Eli calls my name and waves me over.

"I think it would be easier if we just settled this ourselves," Natalie says to me. *Sheesh*. Eli did a number on her.

And fast, too. This must be some sort of record for him. "There wasn't much damage done to my car. But you'll probably need to be towed."

"I have AAA," Eli says. "I'll call them now." He backs away to make the call.

"Are you okay?" Natalie asks me. She's looking at the flakes of dried puke on my leotard.

"I'm okay," I say quickly. "Just got a little carsick."

She nods and smiles slightly. "My sister was the same way before she had my nephew."

I blink. What do her sister and her nephew have to do with me being carsick?

Eli comes back over. "They'll be here in about thirty minutes to take us to the closest mechanic."

THIRTY MINUTES? I want to scream, but I force my mouth to stay closed. What did I think? That after everything I'd still be able to make it to my audition? No way. That ship has puked on itself and sailed.

Tears brim and a sniffle escapes. Eli glances at me, and I walk over to sit on the guardrail because I don't want him to see me cry. The most important day of my life is ruined. This is worse than the night I broke my ankle. Worse than the day Mom told me she wouldn't let me audition for the conservatory.

I wish I could call her now to hear her tell me everything will be okay, but I can't ever tell her about this. I'm about to full-out cry, when Natalie walks over and wraps me in a tight embrace. Her bony arms make the hug a little uncomfortable, but I appreciate it nonetheless.

"Good luck with your family," she whispers before she lets me go.

I stare at her. *"Huh?"*

But she's already walking away and climbing into her indestructible Impala.

Eli goes to put Geezer on his leash, and they both join me at the guardrail. Eli is uncharacteristically silent as he sits down beside me. His baseball cap is back.

"What did you tell Natalie?" I ask.

For a second, he looks sheepish. "I told her that you're pregnant and that's why you threw up."

"WHAT?"

"Not done," he says, holding up a hand. "*And* that you were my girlfriend, and I was taking you to D.C. to propose."

"Eli!" I smack his arm.

"What?! Why else do you think she didn't call the cops or why she isn't going to say anything to her insurance company? It wasn't my best lie, but she was swept up in our fake love story anyway. Now your mom will never find out."

This brings me relief. But still. "I'll miss my audition."

"I know," he says quietly. He reaches down and reties his loose shoestrings. Then he sits up and scratches the back of his neck. I think he's having a hard time looking at me. "What . . . what kind of ballet audition was it? For like a group or something?"

I shake my head and then tell him about Avery Johnson and his conservatory.

"Sounds like you have a crush on this Avery guy," he says. I roll my eyes, and then he gets serious. "For real, though, Chlo. After what happened with your ankle, I didn't know you still took dance so seriously. I'm glad you do."

For once he's trying to be nice, but him bringing up my ankle only makes me angrier. "There are a lot of things you don't know about me anymore," I snap.

He frowns and starts to say something else, but the tow truck finally arrives to take us away.

Eli picks up Geezer and sets him down in the cab of the truck and then we both climb inside. I'm squished against the window, but that's fine. I can turn my head as I cry instead of facing forward.

One of my favorite ballets is *The Dying Swan*, a solo piece that is only danced by the most esteemed ballerinas. As the title suggests, it tells the story of a swan that is dying. The choreography is made of upper-body and arm movements, with small and subtle footsteps. Although the piece is short, it's both powerful and beautiful. It's always been my dream to dance this. So it's ironic that I feel like a dying swan, but there is no power or beauty in this moment.

"Are you okay?" Eli whispers to me.

I pretend not to hear him.

Chapter 5

Game Plan

It's going to cost $2,500 to fix my car. $2,500 that I don't have. I'm sobbing so hard, Jay Sanchez, owner of Sanchez & Sons, comes from behind the counter to console me.

Stop crying, I tell myself. But then I think *Mom* and *ballet* and *Avery Johnson* and *no audition* and TWENTY-FIVE HUNDRED DOLLARS. My eyes turn into waterfalls, too many tears for me to catch.

"Chlo," Eli says, softly laying his hand on my shoulder.

"I'm okay." I hate that I'm having a freak-out in the middle of this mechanic shop, where I can barely hear myself think over the sound of the other mechanics shouting to each other. They keep walking by, glancing at the damage to my car and whistling under their breath. Geezer won't stop sniffing around me because he can smell my puke-covered leotard. I wish I could fold into myself and disappear. This is humiliating.

"You're going to need new parts," Jay says. "Twenty-five hundred is the best I can do. I'm sorry."

Before I can plead with him about payment plans or offer dance lessons to a granddaughter or niece in the place of money, Eli pulls out his wallet and shows Jay a shiny silver credit card.

"We'll put the bill on here," he says.

"Wait, what?" I blink. "Eli, you can't pay for this."

"*I'm* not paying for it."

"What is that supposed to mean?"

"My mom gave it to me for emergencies," he says. "Don't you think this counts as an emergency?"

If I weren't trying to keep Mom from finding out that we crashed my car, I would definitely not let Eli charge $2,500 to his credit card on my behalf. But I am trying to keep Mom from finding out that we crashed my car, so I nod and keep my mouth shut.

Jay tells us that since he will have to order the parts, the soonest he can have the car ready is Monday.

"MONDAY?" I shout. *Really, what is up with me and all the shrieking today?* "What are we supposed to do until Monday?"

"There's a motel about a mile from here," Jay says. He must feel really bad for us, because he offers to give us a ride, and he doesn't complain when Geezer farts loudly in the back seat.

Eli uses his credit card to pay for our room, which luckily

is in the back, so we can easily sneak Geezer inside without anyone seeing. There are two double beds with mustard-yellow blankets, and a lamp that flickers like it's close to death. It smells like mothballs and hopelessness.

Eli sets his duffel bag down, claiming the bed closest to the door. Geezer hops up to lie beside the bag, and I slide past them and sit on the edge of the other bed. Eli pulls his pack of cigarettes out of his back pocket and shakes one loose into his palm.

"I'm gonna go for a smoke," he says. "Can you watch Geez for a minute?"

I nod and as soon as he's gone, I shut myself in the bathroom, ignoring Geezer as he sniffs at the door.

I'm unrecognizable when I look at my reflection in the mirror. My bun is coming undone, my edges are frizzy, and my cheeks are dry. I won't even comment on my ruined leotard. I run hot water and use a washcloth to scrub off the leftover puke.

It's 2:03 p.m. Right now I should be inside the Washington Ballet's studio, dancing my way into my future. I shouldn't be sitting on the cold bathroom floor, leaning against the tub in a random motel room in Delaware.

This was my only chance, and I screwed it up. I thought everything aligned so perfectly today because I was meant to make it to this audition, but I was wrong. If I would've kept my nerves together, I wouldn't have thrown up and we wouldn't have had that accident.

Even if by some miracle I found a way to D.C., by the time I got there, the auditions would be over. Avery Johnson and his team would probably be on their way to Raleigh for the next audition on Wednesday.

Wait . . . the next audition is in Raleigh on Wednesday. And Mom will be gone until Sunday. If I go to the audition, I can drive straight home afterward, and she'll still have no idea!

I hop up on my feet at the same time that Eli knocks on the bathroom door.

"Can I come in?" Eli asks.

"No—"

He's already opened the door, poking his head inside.

"I could have been naked," I say, irritated.

"But you aren't." He crosses the bathroom with Geezer on his heels and sits on the toilet-seat cover. "Good. You're done moping."

"I wasn't moping." I cover my nose because he smells like cigarettes. "Can you stop smoking? It's disgusting. When did you even start?"

He waves his hand in dismissal. "We need to come up with a game plan for the next few days until the car is fixed."

"*We* don't need to do anything. I already have a plan."

He grins. "Oh yeah, and what's that?"

"I'm going to the audition in Raleigh on Wednesday." I cross my arms over my chest. "You can figure out your own way to get to your dad's."

His grin widens.

Oh, God. Now we're both going to North Carolina.

"Well, if you're driving to the same state my dad lives in, why wouldn't I want a ride?" He leans forward and clasps his hands in prayer for the second time today. "Look, I'll even drive. You know you don't want to because you're afraid of the highway."

I make a face. "I'm not *afraid*." He snorts. I need to become a better liar. "And look where your fabulous driving has gotten us."

"I wouldn't have crashed if you hadn't *thrown up on me*."

"I wouldn't have thrown up if you hadn't stressed me out so badly! I've never known someone who could literally make another person nauseous."

I would never tell him that I've felt nervous about my dancing since I broke my ankle, which was also his fault, truthfully. It all goes back to him.

"This sounds like a chicken-or-egg situation," he says.

"What?" I shake my head. What is he *ever* talking about?

"I'm paying for the car repairs," he says, bouncing his knees, growing visibly impatient. "You didn't even say thank you, by the way."

"You didn't give me a chance!"

"Okay. Well, I am now." He leans back and crosses his legs at the ankles, waiting.

I feel like there's thick, hot sand on my tongue. I would rather swallow it than say thank you, especially if this is the way he wants to go about receiving gratitude. But I force the words out. "Thank you."

"See, that wasn't so hard," he says. "Now, I promise that Geezer and I will be on our best behavior if you let us go with you."

I look down at Geezer, who is curled up at Eli's feet. Eli is annoying, but what kind of person would I be if I just abandoned him here in Delaware with his old dog? Plus, I *really* don't want to drive. Especially not after the accident we just had.

Again, I can't believe that I'm about to say these words. "Fine. You can come with me."

"Thank you, thank you," Eli says, getting down on his knees to grovel at my feet.

"Stop that." I push him away and he laughs.

"But what will your dad say?" I ask. "Isn't he expecting you today? And did you ever call your mom to tell her you found a ride?"

"My dad only cares if I make it to the college tour on Saturday. My mom knows I'll get to his house eventually."

He stands up and Geezer rolls to his feet. "This is all happening for a reason, you know."

"*What* is happening for a reason?"

He waves his hands in the air. "The car accident. Us being stuck here. Going to a different audition. It's all happening for a reason. We just don't know why yet. So we should probably relax."

I roll my eyes. "Who knew you could be so philosophical?"

"I did. Let's go find something to eat."

On cue, my stomach grumbles, reminding me that it's empty.

"But first, let's change," he says. "We both smell like puke."

Eli lets me borrow one of his T-shirts and we walk to get snacks and dog food from a minimart around the corner. When we get back to our room, I go outside to call Reina while Eli watches TV. While her campers play movie trivia, she sneaks behind a cabin to talk. As expected, when I give her an update on my trip, she thinks it's absurd that I'm still letting Eli come along. She might even be more upset about that than the actual accident. She doesn't have much time to yell at me, though, because she catches two campers sneaking out to the woods, and she has to hang up.

When I walk back inside, Eli is feeding Geezer bone-shaped doggie treats. Suddenly, it hits me that we'll have to be together for the next four days. This is going to be so awkward.

Eli holds a treat up in the air, and Geezer jumps to get it like a seal in a zoo feeding show. Eli smiles. Not his wolfish one, but relaxed and unguarded. He looks up and aims this smile at me. For a minute, there isn't bad blood between us, no elephant in the room. But, then again, who am I kidding? The elephant is sitting right in between us, intercepting our smiles.

We're still looking at each other. I wait for him to say something. He clears his throat, and I go still. Then Geezer jumps into his lap, biting at the snack bag.

"Get down, Geez," Eli says, gently pushing Geezer until he relents and sits back down on the floor. Geezer lowers his head and looks back and forth between us with a sad pout.

"Here you go with the puppy-dog eyes." Eli hands him one more treat. Geezer gobbles it up with a loud snort like he's a little pig, and Eli laughs hard.

Just like that, the moment where he may have been about to apologize is forgotten.

<hr>

At three a.m., I wake up and stare at the walls, briefly forgetting where I am. When I roll over, I see that Eli is still awake, bent over his sketchbook, moving his pencil in quick strokes. Geezer is curled up at the edge of the bed, snoring his chainsaw snores.

Eli drew something for me once, and it changed the way I looked at him.

But that feels like forever ago. A different Eli and a different me.

Chapter 6

Eli Has an Idea

I've finally made it to my audition. I'm feeling nervous, but not nauseous, which is good. When I line up at the barre to stretch, I notice that my feet feel weird. I look down and see that I'm wearing high heels. The silver strappy ones that I picked out for Homecoming last year. And I'm wearing my Homecoming dress: a lavender halter with a tulle skirt that stops at my knees. How could I possibly have left the house and arrived at the audition wearing this outfit? I look around the room and the rest of the dancers are wearing my dress and high heels, too. *What is happening?*

Avery Johnson walks into the room, and everyone stands at attention. He slowly strolls around the studio, examining each of us. I don't realize that I'm holding my breath until he reaches me and pauses. He crouches down and peers closer at my ankle. He sees the pink scar and grimaces. He tells me that my injury is unacceptable. That I'm not ready to audition on this ankle and I should leave. I plead with him and tell him that I *am* ready. He just has to let me show him. In order to prove myself, he tells me to do a hundred *fouetté* turns. I balk at the request, but nevertheless, run to the center of the floor to do what he's asked. I prep and rise up to whip around, spotting my reflection in the mirror. I only manage two wobbly turns before my ankle snaps and I fall hard on my face. Avery Johnson walks over and stares down at me. He shakes his head and says, "You will never be the dancer you once were."

I wake up covered in sweat.

I've had nightmares since I was little. It's one of the many reasons Mom didn't want to go on vacation without me. Before midterms, I always dream that I show up to class without a pencil and my teacher won't let me take my test. Before a recital, I dream that I've brought the wrong costume or forgotten my pointe shoes at home. For weeks after my accident, I dreamt about falling and breaking my ankle over and over again. Last night's dream was particularly frightening. Especially the disgusted look on Avery Johnson's face, and the way he repeated the same words that my doctor told me.

I'm still thinking about it later as I stand in the women's underwear aisle at Walmart.

In the cart, I already have a brush, comb, and oil for my hair, a new plain black leotard, T-shirts and shorts for the next few days, soap, and lotion. Essentials. Eli, however, doesn't have the same mind-set as me. He keeps wandering around the store and somehow finds me wherever I am, holding a random object that he definitely doesn't need. So far, he's come back with a jar of Nutella, a *Guardians of the Galaxy Vol. 2* DVD, and a plastic inflatable basketball. I'm happy that he's gone for now. I don't want him around while I pick out underwear.

A few feet away, an older woman examines a black bra with cups so big they look like they could carry watermelons. I look down at my own chest, which is tiny in comparison. Just this January, I finally fit into a B cup. Having small boobs wasn't something that I had ever worried about. Some girls had big boobs, and some girls, like me, didn't. It came in handy for ballet. I could always fit any costume without needing alterations. But this year my body is becoming something foreign. When I stand in the studio mirror beside my skinnier, white classmates, my thighs are thicker, my chest protrudes further, and my hips are rounder. Mom says that I'm getting my "woman's body." But I don't know how to feel about that. Sometimes I look down at the bit of cleavage I have and feel happy. Other times I think about how some ballet companies don't accept Black female dancers because our bodies are either too muscular or too curvy. Avery Johnson doesn't seem to care about that. His company has dancers of all shapes and sizes. I can only hope he wants his conservatory to be the same way.

I decide that yes, I will buy the paisley pink underwear. I turn to drop it in the cart and—

"BOO!"

I drop the underwear on the floor. And Eli, who's holding a toy water gun in my face, doubles over in laughter. The older woman picking out bras gives us a disapproving look.

"What is *wrong* with you?" I hiss after I've caught my breath.

"You still get so scared," he says, standing upright. "I guess it's something you'll never grow out of."

"And you're so immature. I guess that's something you'll never grow out of."

"Aww. Thanks."

He glances down at the pack of underwear and raises an eyebrow. I can tell that he's fighting a smile. I turn away so he can't see that I'm blushing. Nothing screams virgin like pink paisley print.

I snatch the underwear from the floor and drop it in the cart. Eli does the same with his water gun.

"You don't need that," I say, taking it out and handing it back to him. "Just like you don't need any of this other stuff."

"Who are you to tell me what I need?" He drops the water gun back in.

Choosing not to start another argument, I push the cart down the aisle and Eli follows behind. I head in the direction of the cash registers because we don't need to spend much more time here. Geezer is sleeping back at the motel room, and I'm nervous about leaving him alone for too long.

"I have an idea," Eli says.

"No."

He blinks. "But you haven't even heard it."

"I'm sure I won't like it."

"Let me tell you and then you can decide."

I don't say anything because I'm choosing to ignore him, but Eli takes my silence as a yes.

"We should try to meet up with Trey," he says.

I slow my walk. "Trey Mason?"

"Yeah. He lives in Delaware."

"I know that," I say. "I just didn't know you were still friends."

He shrugs. "We talk sometimes." Then adds, "And we follow each other on Instagram."

"I follow him, too."

Trey has the kind of Instagram account where he doesn't post any pictures of himself, but he reposts funny videos and screenshots of memes. His profile picture is a caricature, like the ones they draw at fairs and amusement parks. In the drawing his hair is longer, like he might be trying to grow dreadlocks, but that's been his profile picture for almost a year. His hair could be to his shoulders or his head could be shaved, and I would have no idea. I don't know if he's still skinny and short, or if he had a growth spurt like Eli. I don't know if he still likes to eat banana and peanut butter sandwiches for lunch.

We used to text a lot when he first moved, but then he started to spend most of his time getting in shape for the wrestling team. It didn't help that I was already busy with ballet.

By the time Reina moved into his old house and she and I became friends, Trey and I sort of fell out of touch. The most we ever text is to wish each other a happy birthday. Maybe that's why I'm so surprised he's stayed in contact with Eli, the same boy who can't even be bothered to call his mom and let her know he's alive.

We pass the candy aisle and Eli drops a pack of gummy worms into the cart. "I just texted him. He's on spring break, too."

"Okay," I say, not really giving it much thought. I'm more concerned about how I'm going to discreetly put Eli's unnecessary items off to the side once we reach the register.

"He offered to come pick us up," Eli continues. "He doesn't live too far from here."

"Oh." I blink. I guess this is really happening.

The three of us back together again, like old times.

Chapter 7

Promises

The summer after Trey and Eli graduated from the eighth grade, Trey's mom, our middle school principal, got a new job as a superintendent in Delaware. That meant she and Trey were moving to a new state. Even though I'd met Eli first, I'd always felt closer to Trey. And, unlike Eli, Trey didn't argue with me about every single thing. Sometimes we could spend an entire Saturday riding our bikes up and down the same streets without getting bored. Now we'd be separated by highways and state lines. I was sad that entire summer.

A few days before he moved, we were watching television in my living room. It was too hot to do anything outside, and Eli was fishing with his dad, so it was just Trey and me. Mom always blasted the AC during summer, so I curled up in a blanket and fought off sleep. I'd had ballet earlier that morning, and even though I was exhausted, I didn't want to spend one of my last days with Trey sleeping.

But I drifted off anyway, and I dreamt that I walked to

Trey's house, but it was empty. He'd left without saying good-bye. I couldn't believe it. I hopped on my bike and tried to ride down to the main road, hoping to catch their moving van, but no matter how fast I pedaled, my tires would only turn in slow motion. I burst into tears with the horrible feeling that I'd never see Trey again.

I woke up to him shaking my shoulder. "Are you okay?" he asked, frowning at me.

"What happened?" I sat up. My neck and forehead were sweaty.

"I think you were having a nightmare. You kept making this weird whining noise like you were crying."

Mom was the only person who knew about my nightmares. I'd always been too embarrassed to tell anyone else. But this was different. Trey was leaving. I wanted him to know the truth.

"I had a dream that you moved away without saying good-bye."

"I would never do that," he said. "You know that, right?"

"I know. It's just that my dreams get weird like that sometimes." Quickly, I added, "Don't tell Eli. He'll only make fun of me."

"I won't tell him," Trey said. He hooked his pinky finger around mine. "I promise."

I smiled at him. "Thanks."

He sat back and slipped his bony arm around my shoulders. "Who cares what Eli thinks, anyway? You're smart and funny and pretty. Nightmares are probably the only thing he can tease you about."

Smart and funny and pretty?

I blinked. Had Trey always thought those things about me? He'd never told me anything like that before. *No boy* had ever told me anything like that before.

As he kept his arm around me and turned his attention back to the television, I got a new thought. It had never crossed my mind that Trey might like me, or that it would make sense for me to like him. We enjoyed the same things. We were the same height. He'd always thought it was cool that I was a ballerina.

A few weeks before, Larissa let me tag along with her on a trip to the mall. We were sitting in the food court, and a boy who worked at Taco Bell kept staring at her. Whenever Larissa would look up and catch his eye, she'd smile, but he'd look away. They went back and forth like this for a long time, until finally Larissa walked right up to him and asked for his number. I told her that I would be too afraid to ever do something like that. She only laughed and said that the boy doesn't always have to make the first move.

I'd already had Trey's number for ages, so I did what I thought was the next logical step. I sucked in a breath, leaned forward, and kissed him right on the lips.

The kiss lasted for a millisecond. Once Trey realized what was happening, he stood up and stumbled backward, putting his hand over his mouth like I'd just tried to rip it off of his face.

"Chloe . . ." he said, blinking. "I . . . I don't . . ."

Mortified, I burrowed my face in my blanket. My cheeks were on fire. *Of course* Trey didn't like me like that. What was I thinking?!

"I'm sorry," I said quickly. "I just thought, because you said those nice things, maybe you liked me like that, and it would make sense if I liked you like that, too." I was rambling, and Trey just watched, shaking his head. Slowly, he sat down beside me again.

"I *do* like you, Chloe," he said after a few seconds. "You're my best friend. It's just . . ."

"Just what?" I waited for him to tell me all the ways in which I was romantically unlikable.

He looked down and bit his lip. His voice was low, and I had to lean forward to hear him. "I don't think I like girls . . . in that way."

"Oh," I said, a little confused. Then, *"Oh."*

"I haven't told anyone yet." He came to sit beside me on the couch and stared at his hands as he spoke. "I mean, my mom and I talked about it, but I haven't told anyone at school." He lifted his face and his eyes met mine. "Promise you won't say anything?"

"I promise." I scooted closer and hooked my pinky finger around his, just like he'd done with me minutes before.

"But now *you* have to promise that you won't tell anyone that I kissed you."

He choked out a laugh. "I promise."

We were quiet for a few minutes. What do you do after you share your first kiss with your best friend and then he tells you his biggest secret?

Here is what you do: you feel grateful that he was willing to share his secret with you, and you keep it, knowing he'll keep your secrets as well.

"Want to bike to Rita's for some ice cream?" I asked.

Trey smiled, looking relieved. "Sure."

Chapter 8

Reunited and It Feels So Good?

We're standing in front of the motel, waiting for Trey to come pick us up. Geezer is sitting behind me, breathing heavily like something is caught in his throat or nose (nothing is there—I checked). And Eli is standing off to the side, smoking. *Again.*

Today he's wearing a black T-shirt that says FIGHT THE POWER and red basketball shorts. His Phillies cap is fastened tight on his head.

He stomps out his cigarette and walks back over to me.

"Do you ever wear anything else?" I ask, gesturing to his outfit.

He looks me up and down and raises an eyebrow. "You mean like you?"

I look at my white T-shirt and gray Soffe shorts. Okay, so I'm basically dressed the same as him right now. I was trying to be as simple and cheap as possible with the clothes I bought at Walmart.

"I don't usually dress like this," I say. "You know that."

"I'm using my clothes to make a statement."

"And what would that be?"

"That I don't care what people think." He stretches his arms above his head, and I take in how tall he is, how long his limbs have grown. The fact that he has muscles. When he glances over at me, I quickly look away.

"What?" I say, because I can still feel him watching me.

"You never relax." He stands up straight as a rod and juts out his chin. Mocking my posture. "Don't you ever just slouch?"

"No." Ballet has drilled holding my center and keeping the ultimate poise into my brain forever. I couldn't slouch even if I wanted to.

Eli takes a step closer and presses his hands onto my shoulders and upper back, bending them forward. It makes me feel like I have a hunchback. "Doesn't that feel better?" he asks.

"No. Why would anyone want to stand like this?" I say, shooing him away. "And you stink like your stupid cigarettes."

He holds a hand over his heart. "That hurt my feelings. Does everyone know you're this rude? And anyway, I'm trying to quit." He lifts up his shirtsleeve and taps a nicotine patch.

"If you're still going to smoke, doesn't that defeat the purpose of the patch?"

"Everyone has their own process."

"You can't smoke around me," I declare. "If you want to stay on this trip, that's the rule."

He groans. "First you tell me that I can't play my music. Now I can't smoke?"

"I said you can't smoke *around me*." I think of the pictures of blackened and shriveled lungs our teachers used to show in health class. "I don't think you need me to tell you about the dangers of secondhand smoke."

"No," he says flatly. "I don't."

"I don't know why you smoke anyway. Are you just trying to piss off your mom?"

"No," he huffs. "I'm not trying to piss off my mom, and I don't smoke because I think it looks cool. I bummed a cigarette off Isiah one day and decided I liked it, but now I'm trying to quit, because I don't want to die from fucking lung cancer when I'm thirty-five. It was a stupid choice, okay, Chloe? Is that what you want to hear? Does that satisfy you?"

"Stop cursing at me," I snap.

"I'm not cursing *at* you!"

I bet we've set some sort of record for the most fights within twenty-four hours. He stares at me, still frowning. I wonder if my frown is as intimidating. Probably not.

"You should at least carry some cologne with you," I can't help saying.

He sucks in a breath, no doubt getting ready for Smoking Argument: Part Two, when a red Jeep barrels down the road. Geezer sits up, suddenly alert as the Jeep slows down and stops in front of us. The driver lowers his window and leans out to get a better look at us. He's wearing sunglasses, and his arms and shoulders are thick and muscular. His dreadlocks are wrapped in a bun on top of his head.

Who is this guy?

But then this stranger takes off his sunglasses, and I recognize those deep brown eyes and that crinkled smile.

"'Sup, guys?" Trey says, opening his door.

He's still only a few inches taller than me. But he isn't skinny anymore. Not only are his arms muscular, but his legs, too. Even his *neck.*

Eli and Trey do one of those boy handshakes that turns into a hug. Trey only reaches Eli's collarbone. They were both so short and skinny when we were younger that sometimes people got them confused. Seeing them together now is fascinating.

"Damn, bro," Eli says. "I know you said you've been in the gym, but are you there every single day?"

Trey laughs. "Basically." He takes a step back and looks up at Eli the way people stand back to view a skyscraper. "And you're tall as hell. Been eating your Wheaties?"

Eli laughs and shrugs. "Not really."

Actually, Eli would prefer to eat cigarettes for breakfast.

I almost say this, but I don't because Trey reaches out to hug me. He smells good, like cinnamon and minty soap. *Not* like cigarettes.

"Wow," he says when he pulls away. "You look great, Chlo."

"Thank you." The last time he saw me, I had a long neck, knobby knees, and braces. I would *hope* that he thinks I look a lot better now. "You look great, too."

Geezer sniffs cautiously at Trey's sneakers. Trey reaches down and pats his head. "So what are you doing out here?" he asks us.

I tell him about my audition, but I leave out the part about lying to Mom. Eli tells Trey he's going to his dad's house in North Carolina.

"Road tripping," Trey says after we are done explaining. "That's dope. I'm not sure what you're in the mood to do, but there's a party I can take you to."

He unlocks his car doors for us.

"A party? Nice," Eli says, grinning as he climbs into the passenger seat, leaving me to sit in the back with Geezer, who likes to fart whenever he's in a car. "Where at?"

Trey glances at me in his rearview mirror before he says, "It's at my boyfriend's house."

I watch Eli's face, waiting to see his reaction. But he simply nods and says, "Sounds good. I'll finally get to meet him."

"What's your boyfriend's name?" I ask, leaning forward to join the conversation.

"Eric. We go to school together."

"Do you have pictures?"

"Yeah." Trey smiles. He hands me his phone and tells me to look through his camera roll.

There are a lot of photos. I wonder why Trey never posts any of them on his Instagram, and I decide that he might just be a very private person. I pause on a photo of Trey standing arm in arm with a boy who's about his height. The boy has shiny black hair and golden-brown skin. They're standing on the beach, sporting wide smiles. They look happy. Like they're in love.

"He's really cute, Trey," I say, because it's true. "You did a good job."

"Relax, Chlo," Eli says, shifting to look at me. "Eric is taken."

He literally ruins everything.

"Shut up," I say, which, of course, only makes him laugh. But I'm shocked when Trey starts laughing, too. "Don't laugh at him, Trey. He's not funny."

"He can laugh if he wants." Eli lifts an eyebrow, challenging me. Still mad over the cigarette argument, I see.

"Whatever." I lean back and cross my arms over my chest. I'm just going to keep to myself in the back seat. I'd rather smell Geezer's farts than deal with his owner.

"You two haven't changed much," Trey says. "Still arguing like an old married couple."

I pretend to gag. "I'd never marry him."

"I'd divorce you before you could marry me," Eli says.

"That doesn't even make sense!"

"Hey," Trey says, watching me in his rearview mirror. "You still twitch your nose when you're mad."

"SERIOUSLY?" I say.

Eli bursts into laughter.

Chapter 9

Be Social

Trey's neighborhood is a good forty-five-minute drive from the motel. When we get to Eric's house, cars are lined up along the street, but Trey parks in the driveway. He walks inside without ringing the doorbell. There are people scattered throughout the living room and kitchen, drinking beer and lounging all over the furniture in a way that Eric's parents probably wouldn't approve of. Mom would be livid if she saw someone's sneakers on her couch.

Trey leads us to the kitchen, where people are taking shots. I glance at the time on my phone just to make sure that it *is* actually four p.m. I had no idea people did stuff like this during the day. But what do I know? I've never even been to a party like this at night. When I go with Reina to a theater club party, we play Uno and Taboo. Every now and then someone will sneak a bottle of their parents' wine, and that one bottle will be passed around to the twelve or so people who showed up.

Two girls squeal when they notice Geezer. They run over to pet him, and he freaks out and starts barking like he's under attack. The girls scramble backward, but their terror eases as they watch Eli bend down and whisper in Geezer's ear, calming him.

"Your dog is scary," one girl says. She's tall and pale with platinum-blond hair and dark roots. She adjusts the straps on her tank top and isn't discreet about the way she looks Eli up and down.

Eli glances up at her, and when he notices that the girls are appraising him he stands upright and smiles.

"I train him to be tough," he says. And I give him a look, because I wouldn't necessarily call Geezer tough. More like a cranky farting machine.

But who cares what I think, because the girls are giggling, and *ugh, gross*. I am not about to sit around and watch them fawn over the most annoying human on planet Earth.

Luckily, I don't have to, because Trey loops his arm in mine and leads me to the backyard. There are more people outside talking and eating. Someone even brought a wooden table outside for beer pong. I wonder what Reina and the people from theater club would think of this.

I recognize Eric standing by the grill, flipping burgers and hot dogs. When he glances up and sees us approaching, his mouth breaks into a huge grin.

"Hey, babe," he says, stepping away from the grill to give Trey a kiss.

"This is my friend Chloe," Trey says. "The one I told you about."

Oh no. I feel my eyes go wide. What did he tell Eric? That I tried to kiss him when we were younger because I thought he liked me?

"You're the dancer," Eric says.

"Yeah." Relief floods through me. "It's really nice to meet you." I hold out my hand for a shake, but Eric pulls me in for a hug instead.

"You hungry?" he asks me as he places a hamburger on a bun and hands it to Trey, who gobbles it up in two bites.

My stomach growls, and then Geezer brushes up against my leg. I turn around, and Eli is standing behind me. I look over his shoulder, expecting to see at least one of the girls from the kitchen, but he's alone.

"I don't know about her, but *I'm* hungry," he says.

After Trey introduces Eli and we all have a plate of food, we make our way to a cluster of empty chairs. This short trip takes a bit of time because people keep stopping Trey to say hello or ask how his spring break is going so far. It suddenly clicks that this is happening because Trey is *popular.* People genuinely care about how he's doing and what he's been up to. I wonder if he would have been popular like this if he'd stayed in New Jersey.

When we finally sit down, Trey pulls his car keys out of his pocket, and I notice a Penn State key chain. I point to it. "Is that where you'll be going in the fall?"

"Yep, for wrestling," he says. "I didn't really wanna stay on the East Coast for college, but they offered a nice scholarship."

"Well, if you're staying on the East Coast, maybe I can come visit you."

I really regret that we fell out of touch. Trey must feel the same way because he smiles and says, "Yeah, that'd be nice."

"And you and Eli can probably visit each other, too, since he's staying on the East Coast, also," I say.

Trey glances at Eli and quirks an eyebrow. Eli's mouth breaks into a grin.

"Actually, I'm still trying to get my parents on board with clown school," he says.

They both laugh, but I can tell that Eli's is a little forced. Maybe he's embarrassed to talk about how he's going to study to be a lawyer just like his dad.

Eric comes back to the table and asks Trey to come help him at the grill. Trey tells us he'll be back soon, and then there's just Eli and me. And Geezer, of course.

Eli is busy scrolling through his phone. I wait to see if he'll look up and try to start a conversation. He doesn't.

"So . . ." I say once the silence becomes a little unbearable.

He glances up at me. "So . . ." he repeats.

"What happened to your hair?"

He sighs. "I knew that was coming."

"You have a huge bald spot in the middle of your head. You can't expect me not to ask about it."

"Someone shaved it as a joke."

"*What?* Who?"

"Isiah."

"Are you serious?"

"I fell asleep at a party." He tries to shrug it off, but I can tell it still annoys him.

It really puzzles me that Eli quit the basketball team out of the blue and dropped all his teammates to become close with Isiah, the slacker of all slackers. Did he need to change his image that badly? Just like with the smoking, he probably did it to get under his mom's skin.

I say what I've been wanting to say for over a year. "I can't believe you're friends with him."

"I wouldn't really consider Isiah a friend."

"Then why do you hang out with him all the time?"

"We stopped hanging out a while ago."

"Oh," I say, surprised. "I didn't know that."

"There are a lot of things you don't know about me anymore." He repeats the exact words I said to him yesterday. Touché, I guess.

He stands up and pats his pockets. I already know what he's looking for.

"I'm gonna go smoke," he says, tapping a cigarette out of the pack and into his palm. He coaxes Geezer to stand up. "See you later."

"What?" My heartbeat quickens. "You can't leave me sitting here by myself."

"*Well*, I'd invite you to come, but you have that rule about me not smoking around you, so . . ."

"But I don't know anyone here."

"Not true," he says, already backing away. "You know Trey. And now you know Eric."

I glance around hopelessly. Trey and Eric *were* at the grill, but now they're nowhere to be found.

"You look like you're about to face sudden death," Eli says, smiling. I'm glad he finds this funny. "It's not that deep. Just . . . be social." He starts to walk away.

"Eli," I hiss. But I'm long forgotten as he makes his way to the front yard, and the platinum blond with the dark roots falls into step beside him.

Be social. How does one do that? I never have time to really be social because of ballet. And when I do go out, I can always hide behind Reina, who has more than enough to say for the both of us. Now that she isn't here, I'm not sure what to do.

And how is it that both Eli and Trey have grown up to be so popular, while I'm just . . . well, I'm just me. The type of girl who sits alone at a party, awkward and self-conscious.

Luckily, the sun is beginning to set, so I won't be seen sitting alone in broad daylight.

All I need to do is talk to one person, and somehow be charming enough that they will talk to me until Trey or Eli comes back . . . which may never happen with the way things look. But even the thought of doing that makes my palms sweat.

I stand up and start to walk around the backyard slowly, like I'm just minding my business, doing a casual stroll. What I'm really doing is scanning the crowd, trying to catch someone's eye so I can spark up a conversation. About what? I have no idea. But it doesn't matter anyway. Everyone is clustered together in groups. I bet their high school is small like ours, where everyone knows everyone and it's hard to break into cliques.

This is useless.

The good thing is that most people are outside now, so I make up my mind to head inside. If I use the bathroom, that will eat up some time. Maybe when I come back, Trey will be waiting for me.

There's a line for the bathroom downstairs. I wait for a little bit, trying not to eavesdrop on the two girls standing in line ahead of me. But it's hard not to, because one girl is shouting about how a boy named Dave is completely ignoring her, even though she just slept over at his house, and her friend keeps making really disinterested *mhmm* sounds like she's about to fall asleep while standing. All I can think is that Mom would crucify me if she ever found out that I'd stayed overnight with a boy. I will never tell her about sleeping in the same motel room as Eli, even though we were in separate beds.

After a while, I really do have to use the bathroom, and the line doesn't seem to be moving. In a big house like this, there *has* to be another bathroom upstairs. I decide to search for it.

I was right.

The upstairs bathroom is huge. The tub is a large Jacuzzi and there's a half wall that separates the tub from the toilet. There's a window by the toilet, too. This is perfect. I can hide out in here and watch the backyard until I see either Trey or Eli sitting back at our table.

After I use the bathroom, I ease myself down onto the soft plush rug. I pull out my phone and scroll through my timeline. Reina just posted a selfie with a bunch of her theater camp students. She's beaming, and the little kid next to her has his finger stuck in his nose. I start to comment on the picture, then I freeze when I hear the bathroom door open.

Did I forget to lock it?

The voices drift closer and I hear the door close behind them. Someone turns on the sink.

I definitely forgot to lock it.

I start to stand up and announce myself before someone starts doing something . . . private, but I stop when I realize that I recognize the voices. It's Trey and Eric. And they're arguing.

"There are way too many people here," Eric says.

Trey says something back, but I can't really hear over the sound of the running water.

"No, most of these people are *your* friends," Eric says.

Someone turns off the sink. Trey clears his throat. "You're friends with them, too. You didn't care earlier. I don't see what the big problem is all of a sudden. I'm so tired of your on-and-off attitude. Why don't you just say what this is really about?"

"It's about you and your need to invite everybody under the sun every time we decide to have a party," Eric says.

"No, that's not it. You're mad that I'm going to Penn State and not with you to UM. Just say it."

Silence.

I hold my breath like they can hear the sound of my breathing. It's so quiet they just might.

"You know what," Eric says suddenly, "I don't want to have this conversation right now. There's a bunch of people here that *you* invited, and they're probably fucking up my house as we speak. I need to go back downstairs."

"Fine."

The door creaks open. "Are you coming?"

"I'll be down in a few minutes."

From the heavy silence, I can tell that Eric is lingering. "I'm sorry," he says softly. "Can we talk about this after everyone leaves?"

"Yeah," Trey says quietly.

The door closes. Then I hear his footsteps walking toward the toilet, toward *me*. This will be very, very bad. And embarrassing.

But Trey walks right past me and stands in front of the window. His shoulders sag and he lets out a long sigh. I wait for him to look over and discover me, but he doesn't.

He just might stand at the window all night, pondering and brooding.

I clear my throat. Trey snaps his head in my direction and practically jumps out of his skin. "Chloe, what the hell are you doing down there?"

I shrug and smile sheepishly.

He glances at the door and looks back at me. I can tell the wheels are turning in his brain, putting together that I just overhead his argument with Eric.

"I didn't mean to eavesdrop," I say quickly. "I *wasn't* eavesdropping. I just happened to be in the same room while you were having an argument. . . ."

I don't know what I expect Trey to do. But he doesn't get angry. Instead, he sighs and sits down on the rug, leaning his head against the wall with a loud *thunk*. "We had this plan that we'd both go to the University of Miami next year, but then Penn State gave me a wrestling scholarship. I couldn't turn it down. I wanted Eric to apply there, too, but his parents aren't really supportive of the fact that he's gay, so he wants to get as far away from them as possible. He says Pennsylvania is still too close." He looks down at his hands in his lap.

"I'm sorry," I say.

"Lately, he gets mad at me out of nowhere, and I know it's because he thinks that I messed up our plan. But he'll say it's because of different stuff. Like the other day he got mad that I made us late to school, when he's never cared about that before. And today it's because I invited too many people to his house, but he's had even bigger parties than this."

I don't know what to say, so I nod to let him know that I'm still listening.

"I just want him to be honest with me, you know? Lying eats you up," he continues. "It's exhausting and time consuming and only hurts people."

I think about Mom and how I'm lying to her. "I know what you mean."

"I was worried that we'd break up because of the long-distance thing, but it might happen before we even go away." He glances out the window. When his gaze returns to me, he raises an eyebrow. "Why were you sitting on the bathroom floor anyway?"

"I was hiding."

He laughs. "Hiding from what?"

Loneliness. "You left, and then Eli left. I didn't have anyone to talk to, so I just found my way up here."

Trey makes a face but thankfully lets my antisocial behavior slide. "So are you and Eli cool again? I didn't have a chance to ask him."

"No." I snort, then backtrack. "How much, exactly, did he tell you?"

"Not much." He shrugs. "He said you got into a fight

and stopped speaking. He didn't go into a lot of detail, and he only brought it up once. We really just got in touch again recently, like within the past couple months."

"Oh," I say. "Well, yesterday was the first time I'd talked to him in over a year." I pause, realizing I don't feel like going into detail, either. "He's changed a lot since you moved."

Trey smiles softly. "Maybe go a little easier on him. He's been going through some stuff."

I start to ask what he means, but Trey switches topics and says, "So this dance audition is pretty big?"

I nod and tell him about Avery Johnson's conservatory.

"What does your mom think about you going all the way to North Carolina to audition without her? I'm honestly surprised she even let you."

I look away. "She didn't."

"She *didn't*?"

"She's on vacation right now. She thinks I'm staying at my best friend's house."

Trey starts cracking up. I wish I thought it was as funny as he does. Instead, I just feel guiltier.

"I guess that doesn't really surprise me," he says once he's done laughing. "There was always something kinda fierce about you."

"Me? Fierce?"

"Yeah," he says easily. "I mean, only a fierce girl would kiss her friend without any warning at all."

I groan and bury my face in my hands. "I will never live down that embarrassment."

"It wasn't so bad." Trey gently peels my hands away from my face. "I'm lucky you got to be my first kiss. Honored, even. It could have happened at a random party with some sweaty boy whose mouth tasted like stale garlic bread. That was my second kiss."

I can't help but laugh. "Maybe I was fierce then, but I don't know about now. I broke my ankle last year; I just feel different. Sometimes I can't tell if I'm actually not dancing well or if it's just all in my head. Right now, I don't even know why I decided to go to this audition. It's starting to feel a little impulsive and ridiculous."

He shakes his head. "I don't think it's ridiculous."

"I still have those bad nightmares," I say, and he frowns. "I had one about my audition last night."

He's quiet for a moment. "You remember what I used to look like before I moved, right?" I nod. "I was skinny and awkward. You should have seen the coach's face when I showed up at the wrestling tryouts freshman year. He almost laughed me right out of the gym, but I didn't let him. After I made the team, there were times when I felt stupid for joining. The guys I wrestled against were a lot better than me and I doubted myself all the time, but eventually I just had to say fuck it and push those thoughts out of my head because I was never going to get better."

He nods his head at me. "You're having those dreams

because you're doubting yourself, and you have to stop. You've danced *way* longer than I've wrestled," he says. "If I can do it, you can do it. Once fierce, always fierce."

I smile. I don't feel less doubtful necessarily, but I do feel better. He's always had a way of brightening my mood. "Thanks, Trey."

We sit in a comfortable silence. It's like no time has passed between us at all. My life would be so different if he never moved. I wouldn't have been upset when Eli started ninth grade and ditched me. And I would've had someone to show me around the high school once I started, a friendly face to teach me the ins and outs.

But then again, if Trey never moved, I wouldn't have met Reina, because her family moved into his house, and Trey wouldn't have met Eric. And we wouldn't be having this conversation right now.

"What do you say we rejoin the party?" Trey says.

I shrug. I'd rather not, but I let him pull me up anyway, and we head downstairs. The party has found its way into the living room, and a crowd has formed around a boy who looks like he might be dancing, but I'm not really sure because he's just flailing his arms and spinning in a circle. Everyone is cheering him on, though, so it makes me wonder if this is what people around here consider to be good dancing skills. The boy must have been at it for a long time because his cheeks are red, and his Wilson High Wrestling T-shirt is covered in sweat stains.

Trey takes one look at his teammate and rolls his eyes. "He gets drunk and does this at every party." He motions for me to follow him into the kitchen, but the living-room crowd is so thick, we're quickly separated.

As I watch Trey get farther away from me, the dancing boy finally grows dizzy from all his spinning and flailing and begins to stumble. The crowd parts for him and he crashes onto the floor right in front of me. He closes his eyes and groans.

"Are you okay?" I ask, leaning down a little.

He opens his eyes. They're bloodshot. He rolls onto his side, facing me, and groans again.

"Wow . . ." he says slowly, "that's a sick scar. How'd you get it?" I realize he's staring at my ankle. He reaches out a meaty hand and runs his fingers along my scar.

"Uh, it was an accident." I try to pull away, but then he wraps his fingers around my ankle and holds on.

"Hey, wait. Don't leave." He finally looks up at me. "Do I know you?"

"No." I tug away harder, but he still won't let go.

He blinks a few times like he can't see straight. "You sure? I swear I've seen you before."

"No. *Let go, please.*"

"Come on, Ben," another boy says, laughing. "Leave her alone."

I frantically search for Trey, but he's nowhere to be found. Then I spot him and Eric standing in the kitchen entryway.

They're hugging. I want them to make up, of course, but do they have to do it *right now*? I call Trey's name, and he turns around. When he sees me, he and Eric immediately start pushing their way back through the crowd.

"Let go of me," I say to the boy, who I think is named Ben.

"Can you help me up?" he slurs. Then he burps. Oh my God. Is he going to throw up on me? I've already thrown up on myself. Isn't that enough? "And then can I get your number?"

Before I have a chance to tell him that will never happen, two hands grab the back of Ben's T-shirt and yank him up, startling him into releasing my ankle. Then he's shoved back to the ground.

I jump back in surprise. Suddenly Geezer is barking in front of me. What the heck just happened?

"That's her bad ankle, you dumbass," Eli says, standing over Ben.

The entire living-room crowd gathers around us and I wonder where all these people were when Ben wouldn't let go of me.

Eli turns to me. "You all right?"

I nod and look down at my ankle. The skin is red where Ben grabbed me, but otherwise I'm fine.

Seconds later, Trey and Eric are both at my side.

"Are you okay?" Eric asks.

"I'm so sorry." Trey spares a brief glance at his teammate

who's on the ground, moaning. "Ben's an idiot. I didn't even invite him." He turns to Eric. "I swear I didn't invite him."

"It's okay. I'm okay," I say, suddenly feeling exhausted. "Trey, do you think you can give us a ride back now, please?"

"Of course, of course."

We say good-bye to Eric, and we ignore the crowd as we follow Trey outside to his car.

"Eli!"

We all turn around. The blond with the dark roots is running down the driveway. Eli swears under his breath.

"I forgot to give you my number," she says once she's right in front of him.

Eli takes a step backward. "I'll, uh, get it from Trey."

Her face falls. "But—"

"Nice meeting you." He rushes to Trey's Jeep, and he and Geezer quickly climb inside.

She stares, slightly shocked. Then she spins on her heel and storms back up the driveway.

Trey looks at me and raises an eyebrow.

I shrug. "That's typical Eli for you."

But do you know what isn't typical Eli behavior? Him standing up for me.

"Thank you," I say to him once I'm in the car, too.

He shrugs. Nonchalance. Typical Eli again.

I feel sad saying good-bye to Trey as we pull into the motel parking lot. He and Eli say good-bye first, and then Eli leads Geezer away toward our room.

I hug Trey tightly. I'm so happy that I got to see him, even if it was only for a little while.

"I never thanked you for keeping my secret back then," he says.

I pull away. "You don't have to thank me."

"How would you feel if I asked you to make another promise?" he asks. "Let's promise we won't let another three years go by before we meet up again."

We smile at each other. I hook my pinky in his.

"I promise," I say.

"Let me know how your audition goes," he says. "And remember what I said. Once fierce, always fierce."

He beeps his horn as he drives out of the parking lot. I send him good vibes and hope they'll last until the next time I see him. And I really hope that he and Eric can work things out.

Eli is standing at our room door, holding it open for me.

He watches me curiously as I slide past him, inside. "What were you guys talking about?"

I feel myself smile. "Nothing."

Chapter 10

Self-Defense

I wake up gasping for breath, like I've just run a marathon.

I had the dream again. Just like last night, Avery Johnson asked me to do *fouetté* turns while wearing my Homecoming dress and heels, and my ankle snapped. I can still feel the terrifying sensation of falling. I stare up at the ceiling and remind myself that it was only a dream and try to ignore the tight knot that's formed in my stomach. I breathe in and out slowly to the rhythm of Geezer's snores. I sit up and rub my ankle, running my finger over the scar.

Trey told me that if I want the nightmares to stop, I have to stop doubting myself. But he didn't say *how*. When I think of fierce women, I think of Beyoncé and Michelle Obama and Oprah Winfrey. I doubt before a concert or speaking engagement that they have nightmares and wake up sticky with their own sweat.

There's only two days left until the audition. Then these

nightmares will end. But knowing it's so close doesn't make me feel much better.

> Have you left him on the side of the road yet?

That's the text Reina sends me as we're waiting for Jay Sanchez to pick us up and take us back to his shop.

I text back: Nope. He's still here.

> ☹ there's still time. I'll check in again later tonight

I almost tell her about how Eli stuck up for me last night, but it won't make much of a difference. Reina just doesn't like Eli. She thinks he's too arrogant. The type of boy who knows he's good-looking and uses it to his advantage. It doesn't help that when she first moved into Trey's old house, Eli tricked her into believing that Trey and his mom still owned the house and they were going to come back and kick Reina's family out at any moment.

Mostly, though, she doesn't like him because of the way he hurt me.

She texts me pictures of shoe options for prom and asks which ones will look best with her dress. That's all everyone at school is talking about these days. Everyone except me, since I'm not going to prom. I haven't had the best luck with school dances. Plus, Reina is going with a boy named Greg that she knows from theater club, and I don't want to play third wheel.

I wonder if Eli is going. It's his senior year after all. I bet he thinks he's too cool for it, though.

"Did you learn self-defense in P.E. last semester?" he suddenly asks, peeking over my shoulder.

I nearly jump out of my skin. "Don't sneak up on me like that!"

"Did you learn self-defense in P.E. last semester?" he repeats.

I blink. What a random question. "No."

He lets out a frustrated sigh. "Why not?"

"I don't know. I don't even remember it being an option."

"Listen, you need to know how to defend yourself. Especially if you plan on living in New York City. An innocent girl like you is the perfect victim."

I roll my eyes. "You sound like my mom."

"I never thought I'd have anything in common with your mom, but we're both right."

"I'll carry pepper spray."

"What if you can't get to it fast enough?"

"I'll kick him between the legs."

He laughs. "Who said it was a guy?"

"I'll . . . I'll punch her in the boobs." But no, that seems so wrong. Then again, if I'm being attacked, I guess it won't matter what I think is right or wrong.

Eli squares his shoulders. "Let's role-play really quick," he says. "I'm going to try and grab you, and I want you to find a way to protect yourself."

"*What?*"

"I want you to hit me."

"No." I back away. "I don't want to hit you."

"Just try, Chloe." He looks so serious. "This is something you should know how to do."

Knowing that he's right is annoying. "Fine."

"Okay," he says, and before I have a second to prepare myself, he lunges for me. I try to twist out of his grasp, but it's hard because his arms are so long. The last time we were this close, we were in middle school and I was wrestling him in my front yard because he unzipped my book bag and stole my Doritos. I didn't feel butterflies then, and I hate that I feel them right now.

I elbow him in his side, and he loosens his hold a little bit, but not that much. I wriggle around in his arms until he finally lets go. Geezer trots around us, wagging his tail. He probably thinks we're playing a game.

"That was bad," Eli says. "Try again."

This time when he reaches for me, I back away and punch him in his shoulder with all my might. I use so much force that I hurt my knuckles. Eli barely flinches. It only slows him down for a second until he has his arms around me again.

"You're not playing to your strengths," he says when he lets me go.

"What does that even mean?!" Now I'm agitated. And why haven't those stupid butterflies gone away?

"You know your body," he says. "Where are you the strongest?"

I think about this for a second, and . . . of course, my legs! All that ballet muscle.

This time when Eli comes at me, I wind my left leg back and kick him hard, right in his shin like I'm doing a *grand battement*. He bends over and winces. *"Shit."*

"Sorry!" I gasp. "You told me to do it!"

"I know, I know." He groans a little, rubbing his shin. "It's fine. Good job."

Of course this is the moment that Jay Sanchez drives up. He rolls down his window, concern written all over his face.

"Are you okay?" he says, but he's looking at me. He probably thinks I kicked Eli for a reason, that he did something bad to me.

"I'm fine!" My voice is high and nervous. "We're fine!"

Eli stands up and forces a smile. I can tell by the way his mouth twitches that his shin still hurts. "We were just messing around."

Jay still looks a little skeptical. "Okay," he says slowly.

He takes us back to his shop, and the bumper on my car is all fixed. As I'm inspecting it, Eli pays Jay with his credit card.

"So," he says when we're finally in my car. "Where to now?"

It's weird that I can go anywhere I want without having

to ask Mom. Where *do* I want to go? How do normal people behave when they have this kind of freedom?

I search my brain for ideas but come up empty. "I honestly don't know."

"That motel we just stayed in was trash," he says, tapping his fingers against the steering wheel. He looks over at me. "I know a better place in D.C. It's mad fancy. I stayed there before with my dad."

"I've still never been to D.C.," I say. "I'd be down for that."

"D.C. it is." Then he says, "Wait, one more thing. I want to suggest an amendment to the rule about not playing my music in your car."

I raise an eyebrow. "I'm listening."

"What if we make a combined playlist, some of the music both of us like?"

I mull this over. I don't want to spend the next couple hours listening to commercials and Top 40 stations, either.

"I guess that's all right," I say.

It takes a bunch of back and forth, but when we stop to fill up the gas tank, we come up with a pretty decent playlist. Eli picks songs from Kendrick Lamar, Jay Z, and Chance the Rapper. I add some Jorja Smith, Frank Ocean, and Solange. The first song that plays is Solange's "Losing You." Eli cringes, and I wait for him to throw another fit, but he eventually starts to nod his head along to the beat. I guess Solange has that effect on even the most bothersome of people.

Then it's: so long, Delaware.

Chapter 11

Our Nation's Capital

There are lots of tourists in D.C., but I didn't expect to see so many businesspeople. The men are dressed in sleek suits and carry briefcases, and the women brush past us in their high heels. I pull self-consciously at the hem of my Soffe shorts and wish my sneakers weren't scuffed. I wish I were wearing one of my sundresses. I feel so out of place.

Eli barely seems bothered in his basketball shorts and T-shirt. He's leading the way up Third Street, urging Geezer to keep up his good pace. He starts to slow his walk, and we pause at the corner of Third Street and Madison Drive.

"Let's walk up Madison," he says.

"What's this way?" I ask, although my question is answered when I see the museums lined up ahead of us.

"The National Mall."

"Mall?" I repeat, thinking of department stores and food courts. "This doesn't look like a mall to me."

He laughs a little. "Not *that* kind of mall."

We hover over a map that we grabbed. I want to do all the things, see all the museums. We're only here for one day so we need to act fast. I suggest we see the National Museum of African American History and Culture, the Holocaust Memorial Museum, and the Museum of American History. In that order.

Eli scratches the back of his head. "Yeah, there's just one problem. We have Geezer with us."

"Oh yeah." Well, that excitement was short-lived. I could just leave them, but it's not fun going to museums alone. "There are lots of memorials outside. If we stick to those, we'll still have a lot to see."

We walk to the Washington Monument. It looks like a gigantic white pencil pointing up toward the sky. I take a picture and almost post it on Instagram, but then I remember I shouldn't leave any evidence that this trip ever happened.

We pass by the reflecting pool, and I watch as two little kids make wishes and throw their change into the water. I dig in my bag and throw a nickel into the pool, wishing for acceptance to Avery Johnson's conservatory. I probably should have wished for Mom not to be mad at me once she finds out what I've done behind her back.

Eli snorts when I catch up to him. "You really believe that throwing change into water will make your wishes come true?"

"It can't hurt," I say.

"But you don't believe in my philosophy that everything happens for a reason?"

"Nope."

He smirks and shakes his head like I'm just a silly girl, which annoys me.

Before he can say anything else, I pick up my pace. "Let's walk faster. There's still a lot I want to see."

We come upon the steps of the Lincoln Memorial. It's definitely the most crowded spot on the National Mall. We climb the steps until we're standing on the middle platform. I turn around and look at the reflecting pool and the Washington Monument in the distance. This reminds me of that scene in *Forrest Gump* when Forrest is giving his speech on the Vietnam War, and then Jenny, the love of his life, runs across the reflecting pool, calling his name. It's one of Reina's favorite movies. I take a picture of the view and send it to her. She texts back, JENNY! *Forrest voice*. I laugh.

"What's funny?" Eli asks.

"Nothing. Forrest Gump," I say.

He blinks and tilts his head to the side. "Why are you so weird?"

"Why are *you* so weird?" I push past him and pause in front of the inscription on the ground dedicated to Martin Luther King Jr.

I HAVE A DREAM
Martin Luther King Jr.
The March on Washington
for Jobs and Freedom
August 28, 1963

"I'm going to the MLK Memorial next," I say. I don't wait for Eli and Geezer to catch up.

But I regret my fast pace once I reach the memorial, because it's a good walk from the other parts of the National Mall, and by the time I get there I'm a little winded. Poor Geezer is so tired of walking that he plops right on the ground to take a break and tourists have to maneuver around him.

The memorial is a statue of Martin Luther King Jr. carved out of a mountain. His arms are crossed over his chest, making him look assured and prepared. I stare up at his large stone face and try to imagine what advice he'd have for me about my audition.

Eli walks up beside me and pulls out his sketchbook. In fast, deliberate strokes, he begins drawing the statue. His art style is still the same: realistic and detailed. It's like the sketch he drew of my face last year. When he handed it to me, the likeness was so exact. That was when my crush was born. I had no idea back then that I was setting myself up for failure.

When he notices me looking over his shoulder, he quickly closes his sketchbook and narrows his eyes at me. He was like that when we were kids, too. He never wanted anyone to see what he was drawing.

"Stop being nosy," he says. "Can we eat now?"

"Yeah," I say, turning my face away. Even though there's no way he'd know I was thinking about the stupid crush I used to have on him, my face feels hot.

We stop at a falafel food truck and find a place to sit under a tree in a nearby field. Eli pulls bowls for water and food out of his duffel bag to feed Geezer. After I finish eating, I lean back in the grass and close my eyes. The sun is shining, and a cool breeze blows by us. I haven't felt this free in . . . well, in forever.

Just imagine, if I get into the conservatory, I can lie on the great lawn in Central Park and feel this kind of freedom every day. Freedom I won't be able to experience if I stay home with Mom for the rest of my life. I pull out my phone and stare at my screensaver. It's a picture of us before last year's winter recital. We're hugging each other and smiling into the camera. When we're side by side like this, we still look alike, but while her face is a little flatter and round, I have my dad's cheekbones and pointy chin. She told me that his cheekbones were the first beautiful thing she noticed about him.

She says that falling in love with my dad and having me are the best things that ever happened to her. For years, all we've had is each other, but now she has Jean-Marc, too. I really hope she's actually relaxing and enjoying her vacation with him.

Eli pokes me in the arm, and I open my eyes. "I gotta go smoke. Watch Geezer for me?" He doesn't wait for an answer and takes off across the field, pulling out a cigarette along the way. I think back to how Trey said Eli was going through some stuff. Is that the real reason he started smoking? And what "stuff" is happening with him? I wouldn't even know how to go about asking Eli for an explanation. He'll probably just tell me to mind my business.

I turn my attention to Geezer and pat his head. Instead of grumbling, he actually nuzzles up against me.

When Eli returns, he looks a lot more relaxed now that he's had a cigarette. He plops down beside me and smiles.

"My mom just called me," he says. "I didn't answer and texted her instead. She hates when I do that."

I roll my eyes. "You'll win Child of the Year for sure."

"You're one to talk," he says. "Have you figured out how you're gonna tell your mom about your audition?"

"No, but I have time to think about it. And who knows if I'll be accepted. I might not even have to tell her."

He leans forward. "Let's role-play. You be you, and I'll be your mom. Pretend you already got accepted, and tell me about your audition."

I frown. "What is it with you and role-playing?"

Ignoring me, he says, "Hey, Chlo," in a weird, high-pitched voice that definitely doesn't sound like Mom's. He props his chin in the palm of his hand. "You wanted to talk to me about something?"

He bats his eyes—something Mom never does—and waits.

I know he won't let this go until I play along. Sighing, I say, "Mom, do you remember over spring break when I told you I stayed at Reina's?" Eli nods. "Well, I didn't actually stay there."

He gasps. "*What?* Where were you?"

"I can't do this, Eli! It's too hard to take you seriously."

"Eli?" he says in his high-pitched voice. "I don't see Eli here. It's me, your mom. Carol Pierce."

His earnest expression makes me want to laugh, so I look away as I say, "I went to an audition for Avery Johnson's conservatory."

His eyes get wide. "WHAT? How could you do this behind my back?! You're a terrible daughter! TERRIBLE."

The people sitting near us look over, alarmed. I can't stop laughing.

"Be quiet," I whisper. "You're embarrassing me."

He continues to pretend he's Mom. "So what happened? Did you get into the conservatory?"

I think about my dream last night. The way my heart sank once I fell over. The sound of my ankle snapping. Even in this pretend situation, I can't bring myself to say yes. I look away. "I don't want to role-play anymore."

I can feel Eli staring at me. His voice returns to normal when he asks, "Are you nervous?"

"No," I lie.

"You shouldn't be, right?" he says. "Aren't you really good? That's what my mom and Larissa always say. My mom is still pissed Larissa quit ballet forever ago." He starts to laugh. "Can you believe that?"

"Yes, I can." I try to change the subject. "What's the name of the hotel we're staying at?"

"I forget," he says. "But wait, you must still be really good, because otherwise you wouldn't be going through all of this trouble to audition."

I start to answer him, but then I realize I shouldn't have to explain anything at all. If it weren't for him, I never would have broken my ankle. And I wouldn't be doubting myself.

So I state it plainly, just in case it wasn't clear to him. "I feel this way because of my ankle, you know."

"I know." He averts his eyes for a brief second.

I wait for him to continue, but he just sits there.

"Do you have anything else you want to say to me?" I ask.

"It sucks." He clears his throat. "I wish it never happened to you."

"That's it?" I feel the anger brewing deep in my gut. "Don't you want to apologize?"

He jerks back in surprise. "Apologize for what? It's not my fault you got hurt."

"Not your fault? I wouldn't have been walking to the dance if you'd given me a ride like you were supposed to!" I don't realize I'm yelling until Eli puts his finger to his mouth to shush me, casting a nervous glance around the field. It only makes me angrier. "And you never stopped by after I had surgery to see if I was okay. You ignored me at school and went on about your life while I struggled to get back to ballet, and all you can do is sit here and say *it sucks*? Yes, it sucks because of you!"

I jump up and storm away from him. I don't even know where I'm going. I can't remember where we parked.

"Chloe!"

I turn around and see Eli waving his arm, beckoning me to come back. I start to run and make a random right once I reach the crosswalk, immediately finding myself at the edge of a crowd. Music is playing and people are clapping. It must be a street performance.

Eli calls my name again. This time, he starts to run after me. I push through the crowd so he won't reach me. Maybe I'm being childish by running, but all I know is that I need to get away from him.

Chapter 12

Frenemies: A History

In order to tell the story of how my friendship with Eli fell apart, I have to begin by telling the story of when I felt the closest to him.

In September of my sophomore year and Eli's junior year, his parents officially got divorced. A few months earlier, Eli's dad moved out and got an apartment in Philly to be closer to his office. It was supposed to be temporary. They were trying to work things out in therapy, but they eventually gave up. The night that Ms. Linda came over to give Mom the news, she was armed with a bottle of champagne, ready to celebrate. But instead, they sat in Mom's room with the door closed. I could hear Ms. Linda crying as I did my homework in the kitchen.

Ms. Linda had been at our house for hours by the time Eli came looking for her. Wordlessly, he sat down across from me at the kitchen table. He looked so sad, and I had no idea what to say to him. We could hear the muffled sounds of our mothers' voices above us.

"You know what's funny?" he said suddenly. "All they've ever done is fight. I don't think they ever really loved each other. Why do I feel so surprised that they're divorced now?"

He sighed, long and deep. I was startled when he wiped his eyes. I hadn't seen him cry since we were kids, and back then he used to cry over falling off of his bike or accidentally breaking one of his toys. It was never because of something serious like this. These quiet tears were foreign to me.

I walked around the table and sat down next to him, gently resting my hand on his arm. "I'm really sorry, Eli."

He turned toward me then, and laid his head on my shoulder, surprising me. I sat there frozen, but instinct kicked in and I wrapped my arms around him. He cried quietly, and I kept repeating that everything was going to be okay.

I don't know how long we sat there like that. But eventually we heard the sound of our mothers coming down the steps. Eli pulled away from me, and mumbled a quick "See you at school." Then he and Ms. Linda left.

During school, I never saw him walking down the hallway alone. He was always with some of his teammates, and the most we ever did was acknowledge each other with a quick wave or head nod. But the next morning, there he was, standing at my locker, holding his sketchbook.

"Hey," he said as I approached.

I stared at him. "Hey."

Quietly, he said, "I wanted to thank you for yesterday. For being there for me."

I shook my head. "You don't have to thank me."

"Yes, I do." He ripped out a page from his sketchbook and handed it to me. "Thank you."

I stared at it, marveling at the sketch he'd drawn of my face. He'd captured everything: my beauty marks and the fly-away hairs around my bun. The uneven shape of my widow's peak. "*I* should be thanking *you*. This is beautiful."

He shrugged. "I draw what I see."

I looked up at him, and he held my gaze. My mouth fell open, but no words came out.

Then one of Eli's teammates called his name and clapped him on the shoulder as he walked by.

"I gotta go," Eli said. "See you later."

For the rest of the day, I repeated his words over and over. *I draw what I see.*

He never approached me in school again and he didn't come to my house to talk. But I somehow found a way to glance at his drawing every day, and I felt my stomach tighten whenever I saw him flirting with other girls in the hallway. I always caught him doing that and it had never bothered me before, but suddenly I couldn't stop thinking that those girls didn't know him the way I did. They didn't know he once wore the same pair of Ninja Turtle underwear every day for a week, or that he used to pick his nose *and* eat his boogers when he thought no one was looking.

Then it was late October and time for Homecoming. Freshman year, I'd had ballet early the next morning, so I couldn't go to the dance. But this time, there was no early morning ballet, and I was determined to finally go. Reina helped me pick out a dress and shoes, so all I needed was a ride. Reina was on the Homecoming committee and would be at the gym hours before anyone else, and Mom had to work an evening shift at the hospital. So, unless I took the bus, or walked the mile and a half to school in heels, I was out of options.

The night before the dance, at Mom's suggestion, I walked across the street to ask Ms. Linda if she could give me a ride. I found her sitting on the couch, wearing a bathrobe and slippers with rollers in her hair. Usually, Ms. Linda was nothing if not glamorous. Her high heels clicking against the pavement was one of the sounds of my childhood. Seeing her like this now made me sad.

She was looking through a photo album of her old head shots. She'd moved to New York after high school to be a model, but then she met Mr. Greene and got pregnant, and they moved to New Jersey.

When she finally noticed that I'd walked into the room, she closed the album quickly like she'd been caught doing something bad.

"Hey there, Miss Thing." She smiled and adjusted one of her rollers. "I had a date tonight, but he canceled on me. What can you say? Men, right?" She chuckled to herself in a way that let me know she didn't actually find what she said to be funny. "Do you need something?"

"Yes," I said, remembering the reason I was there in the first place. "Um, I wanted to ask . . . if you have time tomorrow night, do you think you might be able to give me a ride to the Homecoming dance? I hate to ask but my mom has to work, and she thought I should ask you."

Ms. Linda smiled. "Did I ever tell you that I was Homecoming Queen my senior year?"

I shook my head.

"It was one of the best nights of my life." She closed her eyes and sighed. "I have this singles mixer to go to tomorrow night. I won't be able to take you, honey. I'm sorry."

"It's okay," I said, turning to leave. "Thank you anyway."

"Wait. For once, Eli is actually in his room. Ask him if he'll take you."

I froze. I'd been actively trying to get over my crush on him, and talking to him now wouldn't help. Plus, he always thought school dances were stupid. But then I imagined what it might be like to walk to school in the five-inch heels I planned to wear. "I'll see what he says."

I walked upstairs to his room, as I'd done countless times before, but this time was different, of course. In the weeks since he'd cried on my shoulder, he'd changed. He quit the basketball team, started getting close with Isiah, and stayed out as late as he wanted. He even cut school and got caught twice. Ms. Linda had no idea what to do with him. And I had no idea how he'd react to me showing up at his bedroom door.

I knocked, and heard him mumble, "Come in." Tentatively, I opened Eli's door. He was lying in bed with his sketchbook propped up on his chest, blocking me from his view. It was the first time I'd seen him all day. He'd had in-school suspension earlier for skipping class. He'd been doing that more and more lately.

"Mom," he said. "I told you I wasn't hungry."

"It's not your mom."

He moved his sketchbook to the side, and his eyes widened. He sat up. "Oh. What's up, Chloe?"

"Not much," I said, not moving from the doorway. I couldn't remember the last time I'd been in his room, but I knew whenever that was, it didn't smell like cigarettes. His walls used to be covered in posters of basketball players. Now they were bare.

I stepped around a pile of T-shirts in the middle of the floor and sat on the edge of his bed. He placed his sketchbook on the pillow next to his head, and he stared at me, waiting.

"How are you?" I asked.

He shrugged. "Good. You?"

"Fine."

It baffled me that I suddenly didn't know how to talk to him. All I needed was to ask for a ride, and yet I sat there silently, like he was the one who came to see me instead of the other way around.

"Did my mom tell you to come up here and talk to me?" he asked, looking suspicious.

"No. I need to ask a favor." I looked down at my hands. *Just say it. Who cares if he thinks it's stupid?* "Will you give me a ride to the Homecoming dance tomorrow night? My mom has to work a night shift, and Reina has to be at the school by five, and I don't want to be there for three hours until the dance starts, and I asked your mom but she has this singles thing, so—"

"Yeah, sure."

I paused. "Wait. Seriously?"

"I have something to do earlier in the day, but I can swing it," he said. "What time do you need a ride?"

"Seven forty-five?"

"No problem." He leaned back on his elbows. "Do you need me to pick up your date, too?"

"I don't have a date."

"Why didn't you ask me?"

I froze. His lips curled into a smirk. Even as I realized he was teasing, I felt heat creep up my neck. "Shut up."

"I'm serious," he said. Although he didn't seem serious since he was laughing. "I don't look like the Homecoming type?"

"Not really."

"Well, I am. Can I be your date?"

I stared at him. My heart felt like it was going to beat right out of my chest. "Are you being serious?"

"Yeah. My mom will lay off if she thinks I'm doing normal high school stuff. Plus, you and I never hang out anymore. What color is your dress?"

"Lavender," I said, dumbfounded.

He frowned. "I guess I'll look good in lavender."

"You're really going to come?"

"Yeah." He folded his arms behind his head and grinned. "Seven forty-five is kinda early, though. Nobody shows up to dances on time. You know that, right?"

Of course he thought it was uncool to be on time. "I like to be early. What's wrong with that?"

"Nothing." He laughed a little. "I'll be ready by seven forty-five. I promise."

I left his house that night in a daze. I couldn't believe he was really going to the dance with me, and that it was *his* idea. The next night at 7:40 p.m., I sat on my front porch and waited for him. Seven forty-five came and went, and he still hadn't shown up. By 8:15, Reina texted, where r u? I told her I was running a little late and I'd be there soon. When I called Eli, it went straight to voicemail.

By 8:30, he was still a no-show. Then, a little before 9:00 p.m., his Camaro barreled down our block and he pulled into his driveway. I stormed across the street, but froze when Isiah Brown hopped out of the driver's seat. Eli stumbled out of the passenger's side, and like a clown car, boy after boy climbed out of the back seat.

Eli staggered up his porch steps, completely oblivious to

me. Then Isiah turned in my direction to stomp out his ciga-rette. He wolf-whistled, and everyone else turned around, too. I would have been embarrassed if I weren't so angry.

Eli was the last to glance over his shoulder, and when he saw me standing there, fuming, he scrambled back down the porch steps.

His words tumbled out over top of each other. "Chloe. Shit. I forgot. Fuck."

"Where were you?" My voice shook.

"Nowhere. Just . . . around." Now that he was closer, I could smell the alcohol on his breath. I could see how red his eyes were.

"Are you drunk?"

He shook his head so harshly that he stumbled. "No. No, I'm not."

"You're lying."

He shrugged, helpless. "Look, I can still take you. Just give me a sec."

He fumbled in his pockets for his car keys, forgetting that he hadn't even been driving. Isiah tossed them over, but they slipped right through Eli's fingers and landed in the grass. He fell as he bent over to pick them up. Isiah and everyone else laughed. Eli stood up and ran a hand over his face.

"I don't want you to take me," I said. "I'll walk."

What did he think? That I'd go with him in the ashy black T-shirt and jeans he was wearing? That I would go *any-where* with him while he was drunk?

I backed away, and he took a step forward, closing the gap.

"Come on, Chloe. Are you really that mad? It's just Homecoming. Who gives a shit if you miss it?"

"*I* do."

"Homecoming?" Isiah said. "Eli, why didn't you tell us you had to go to *Homecoming*? We didn't have to keep your girlfriend waiting."

The rest of the boys laughed. Eli's cheeks took on a red undertone as he mumbled, "She's not my girlfriend."

Half of me was upset that he was embarrassed they'd called me his girlfriend. The other half was upset because my night didn't have to turn out this way. I could've been at the dance by now, but he'd insisted on coming with me, and he'd broken his promise. I couldn't believe I'd let myself get excited to hang out with him again.

I felt the anger boil inside of me. The words rolled off of my tongue before I could stop them. "I don't know why you bothered to ask to be my date," I said. "Or why I agreed to let you come with me. I wouldn't be able to stand spending an entire dance with you."

Isiah and the other boys kept laughing. Eli stared, wide-eyed.

"You're the worst," I continued. "Don't bother talking to me ever again."

Eli opened his mouth. He closed it. He had nothing to

say. When I turned around and began walking toward school, he didn't try to stop me.

I didn't make it too far before my feet began to feel like they were on fire. The zigzag straps on the heels pinched my toes, and I felt blisters forming on the balls of my feet. I was so blinded by anger and the ridiculous pain that I didn't even realize I'd come up on the busy intersection near school. When the light turned red, I did one quick glance in both directions and stormed across the street. When I was halfway to the other side, a car sped toward me. My heart pounded in my chest as I sprinted the rest of the way. And because five-inch heels aren't meant for running, I tripped over the curb, and my ankle cracked as I fell.

Then I felt the worst pain ever.

The car that almost hit me pulled over to the side of the road, and a pizza delivery guy hopped out to ask if I was okay. He tried to explain that he was rushing to deliver a pizza on time, and that he couldn't see me until he got closer. He didn't even have his headlights turned on. Later, I'd be furious that he almost ran me over just so he could deliver some pizza, but in the moment, I could only yell about my ankle and ask him to take me to the hospital where Mom worked. She met me in the lobby, completely frantic. She shouted at me, wanting to know what happened, why I wasn't at the dance, and why the heck a pizza delivery guy dropped me off, but I could barely answer her. My ankle was bent at a scary angle and it was so red and swollen it looked like there was an egg grow-ing inside of it.

The pain was getting worse, but I didn't freak out yet. Not until I got an X-ray and heard the word *fractured*. Then I realized how bad it was. I wouldn't be able to dance. And then I couldn't stop crying. My thoughts turned back to Eli. This was all his fault.

What's worse is that he didn't even care enough to apol-ogize afterward. Not when I came home in a cast. Not after I had my surgery a week later, and not when he saw me in school, hobbling around on crutches. He didn't say a word to me at all. I found the picture he drew of me and ripped it into shreds.

Saturday was the first time he'd spoken to me since Homecoming. We just spent two and a half days on the road together, and he still hasn't apologized. Maybe he never will.

Chapter 13

The Radcliffe Hotel

I can still hear Eli calling my name as I maneuver my way through the thick D.C. tourist crowd and make it to the center. There's a group of boys who are dancing. One boy is popping and locking and moving his body in ways that I never could. Two boys are doing flips and tricks off of each other's backs, and the fourth boy walks around with a hat, smiling as people drop money into it. Then three of the boys line up and crouch down. The pop-and-locker takes a running start, jumps over the first two and steps on the third boy's back to launch himself into a somersault. He lands in a half split, and the crowd erupts into applause. They can't be older than twelve or thirteen. I envy the way they look so comfortable moving their bodies. I haven't felt that way in so long.

The boy with the money hat opens his arms wide. "We'd like for some of you lovely people to join our show and try some tricks. Any volunteers?"

Hands shoot up in the air, mostly from little kids. Each

boy goes out into the crowd to grab a volunteer. They mostly pick the kids and eager tourists who don't speak English. The popping-and-locking boy seems to be more selective. I stare at the picture of Biggie on his T-shirt until he gets closer and closer. Until he's standing right in front of me, holding out his hand.

"Would you like to join our show, miss?" he says.

Oh no. This is *exactly* what I get for standing up front.

"No, thank you," I say politely, backing up and stepping on someone's foot in the process.

"Aww, come on, don't be shy." He continues to hold out his hand.

The people to my right and left start encouraging me to join him. I really wish this boy would move on to someone else, but he stands there smiling at me. I could just flat-out say no, but I don't want to be mean.

There's no way I'm doing this. People get hurt all the time when they least expect it. Look at what happened to me and my ankle. Or, worst-case scenario, people die when they least expect it. Look at what happened to my dad. I'm not saying I'm going to die while attempting a break-dancing trick, but you never know.

God, I sound like Mom.

Either way, I need to get out of here.

"Actually, I have to go," I say.

The boy blinks. "What?"

Feeling bad, I add, "You guys are so great, though."

I push my way through the crowd. Once I reach the perimeter, I run right into Eli and Geezer.

"Well, look who it is," Eli says, raising an eyebrow.

I start to push past him, but he grabs my elbow.

"Wait," he says, "before you run away again, I need your help getting our hotel room."

I shake my arm loose. "What do you mean, you need my help?"

⁂

"Okay, boy, promise not to make any sounds, all right?" Eli whispers to Geezer as he places him into his empty duffel bag and zips it closed.

We're doing something really stupid: sneaking Geezer into the Radcliffe, a luxury hotel with a strict no-pets policy. We're lucky that Geezer is small enough to fit inside Eli's duffel bag, otherwise this plan would not fly.

"This is a very, very bad idea," I say as we walk through the hotel lobby doors.

I pause, completely stunned at the high ceilings and chandeliers. The white floors sparkle, and the few antique chairs and couches look like they cost more than all the furniture in my house. Eli doesn't miss a beat. He keeps strolling toward the front desk with the duffel bag holding Geezer slung over his shoulder. I panic when the bag starts to move. Quickly, I catch up to them so no one will see Geezer fidgeting.

A man with a thick mustache mans the front desk. After he's done helping the woman in front of us, he raises his eyebrow slightly as we approach him.

"Good evening," he says. "Welcome to the Radcliffe. My name is Brian. How may I assist you?"

"We'd like a room for the night," Eli says, all confidence. "Two double beds, please."

Brian looks at his computer and makes a *tsk* sound. "I'm afraid all we have left are deluxe rooms with king-size beds."

He tells us the price and appraises us. I can tell from his expression that he doesn't think we can afford it.

"That's fine," Eli says, handing over his credit card.

Brian holds the card and squints at it. He looks up at Eli and raises an eyebrow. "Do you have identification?"

Eli frowns as he takes his license out of his wallet and hands that over, too. Maybe he thinks Eli isn't old enough to book a room. He looks eighteen to me.

Brian stares at both cards for a long time. Long enough for it to look like he's trying to piece together a puzzle instead of checking to see if the names match.

"Is there a problem?" Eli asks.

"No, sir. It's simply company policy to ask for ID when guests use credit cards."

"You didn't do that to the woman who was in front of us," Eli says. "You don't think that's my card?"

Brian clears his throat. "Sir, I would never make that claim."

"Well, that's how you're acting."

I start to tell Eli that we should just leave and find another hotel, but then Geezer starts whining. I pretend to have a coughing fit so that no one will hear him. I bend over and act as if I'm hacking up my lungs like an old smoker.

"Goodness, ma'am, are you all right?" Brian says, looking alarmed.

Eli pats my back. "She's fine. Just getting over a bad cold is all."

As soon as Geezer stops whining, I stop coughing. My throat feels raw and sore.

"So, we'll take the deluxe king room," Eli says to Brian firmly, like he's waiting for a challenge.

Brian finally swipes Eli's credit card and hands us our keycards. We rush toward the elevator, and the second the doors close, I partially unzip the top of the duffel bag so Geezer can poke out his head. The first thing he does is lick my cheek.

"That guy was a dick," Eli says. Then he turns to me and smiles. "But this was a brilliant plan, was it not?"

I stare straight ahead and ignore him. If it's not an apology coming out of his mouth, I don't want to hear anything he has to say.

Chapter 14

The Nobleman

Once we're in the room, Eli unzips his duffel bag all the way and Geezer jumps out. When Eli tries to pet him, he shifts away, clearly upset that he was put in the bag in the first place.

I walk around the room, touching the champagne-colored curtains and the gigantic television. If we break anything in here, it will probably take our life savings to pay it back. I kick off my sneakers and start to walk toward the bed, and that's when it hits me: Eli and I will both have to sleep here. This is nothing like the times we napped on the same couch when we were younger. We're practically adults. Actually, Eli *is* an adult. He's eighteen, and he smokes cigarettes. And I can't stand him.

"What's wrong with you?" he asks. He's looking at me funny.

I realize I've been standing in the middle of the room, staring at the bed. I must look like a weirdo.

"Nothing." I grab my bag and fish out my pajamas. Without saying anything else, I walk away to shower and change.

After I brush my teeth and wrap my hair, I walk out of the bathroom and Eli passes me on his way to shower. He looks at my bonnet and grins. I can tell he's about to make a joke, so I hold up my hand before he can speak. "Be quiet," I say.

His grin widens. "I wasn't going to say anything."

I ignore him as I walk to the bed and sit up by the pillows.

When he comes out of the bathroom, he's changed into a new pair of basketball shorts and a fresh T-shirt. I still think his bald spot looks funny, but I don't say anything. He sits pretzel-style at the edge of the bed and starts flicking through television channels. Even from behind, his profile is striking. How annoying.

When Geezer shuffles over and lays his big head against my thigh, I focus all my attention on scratching his head and pretending that Eli isn't here, but I can feel the moment he turns around to glance at me.

"You know what," he says suddenly, "this bed feels pretty bouncy. I bet these springs don't even make a sound."

In one fluid motion, he hops up and bounces lightly, making Geezer and me wobble.

"You're going to break the bed," I warn.

"I don't weigh nearly enough to break the bed." He

bounces again, higher this time, and then keeps bouncing at a steady rhythm.

Geezer grumbles and leaps off of the bed, annoyed. Every time Eli lands, he makes me bounce a little, too. He's too tall to be doing this. He could knock his head into the ceiling. Now *that* would be funny.

"Come on," he says eagerly, holding out a hand for me.

I shake my head. "Will you sit down?"

"Not until you try it, too." His hand is still extended. He wiggles his fingers and smiles.

"No."

He shrugs. "Suit yourself."

The bed is so huge that he begins bouncing around me in circles.

"Watch this," he says. He falls onto his back and bounces right up onto his feet in seconds. "True athleticism."

I want to wipe the smug smile off of his face. "I can do better than that."

"I doubt it," he says.

This is what makes me get up. I go to the corner of the bed and tell Eli to move out of the way. I do a little *chassé* and I leap into a *pas de ciseaux*. It's nicknamed the scissor kick, because my legs slice past each other before I land.

Eli stops bouncing and looks at me in awe. "How the hell did you do that?"

I shrug. "True athleticism."

"I can do that, too." With a determined look on his face,

he jumps in the air, but his legs never scissor. They do a weird flailing swipe. He doesn't look graceful at all. Miss Dana would scold him out of her studio.

"Oh my God," I say, laughing. "That was terrible."

He tries again and almost stumbles onto the floor. I laugh even harder, and then Geezer starts running around the bed, barking at us.

"*Shhh, Geez!*" Eli jumps down and tries to calm Geezer, who is beating his tail against the carpet.

I plop down in the middle of the bed. Eli and I look at each other like we're waiting for someone to bang on our door and throw us out of the hotel for having a dog.

After a few minutes of silence, Eli sighs and I let out a breath. Just as I start to whisper, "That was close," our room phone rings.

"*Shit,*" Eli says. "Just ignore it."

"No. What if someone knocks on our door to see what we're doing? We have to pretend everything's normal." I crawl over to the phone and take in a shaky breath before I answer. "Hello?"

"Good evening, this is Brian from the front desk."

"Hi," I squeak.

Eli looks at me with wide eyes, mouthing, *Who is it?* I whisper that it's the front desk, and he runs a hand over his face.

"We've received a few complaints from guests on your floor," Brian continues. "They said they heard what sounded

127

like a dog barking. I want to remind you that bringing animals into our building is against our policy and would result in a fine."

"Oh! That was just me," I say quickly. "We're playing a card game and whenever I win, I get so excited that I start barking. See . . ." And then, to my own horror, I bark over and over again like a puppy.

Eli starts cracking up and he rolls away, laughing so hard he has to cover his mouth.

"Um . . . all right," Brian says hesitantly. "Please make sure to keep the noise to a minimum. We would appreciate it if you didn't disturb the other guests."

"Of course. Thanks, Brian."

Eli is still laughing when I hang up the phone. Tears are gathering in the corners of his eyes.

"I can't believe I just did that!" I say.

Eli climbs back onto the bed. "That was fucking hilarious."

Things don't feel as awkward as before. I wonder if that's why Eli started jumping on the bed in the first place. Maybe things were feeling awkward for him, too.

"I did try to come see you after your surgery," he says, catching me off guard. "It was the day you came home from the hospital. Your mom told me you weren't having any visitors."

I stare at him for a second. "She never told me that."

He laughs, harsh and short, like that's what he expected me to say. "Of course she didn't. And I knew for a fact that you were having visitors, because Reina had just left before I walked over. Your mom just didn't want me to see you."

I shake my head, confused. "But why would she do that?"

"She hates me," he says matter-of-factly, shrugging.

"No, she doesn't."

"Yes, she does. You think you'll only get in trouble for going to the audition? Nah, you'll really be in some shit once she finds out you've been with me this whole time."

"She doesn't hate you," I repeat. "I just think that her opinion of you is biased. Your mom always complains about you to her."

"Yeah, well, my mom also exaggerates *a lot*."

"Maybe," I mumble.

I'm still trying to process this revelation. He came to see me. And my mom never said anything about it. Why would she keep something like that from me? I'm starting to feel bad for the way I yelled at him earlier.

He leans closer, and I don't back away.

"I know you're mad at me," he says softly. "You've been mad at me for a long time."

My eyes are drawn to his lips as he lowers his voice.

He continues, "And I can see why you're upset."

Has he always had such a nice mouth? I can't look anywhere else.

"But you breaking your ankle really wasn't my fault," he says. "Can't we just agree to disagree?"

I snap out of whatever spell he cast over me. I lean back and narrow my eyes at him. "No," I say. "We can't."

He sighs as I scoot away to the top of the bed and get under the covers.

In the ballet *Giselle*, a young peasant girl meets a nobleman who is pretending to be a commoner. Not knowing that he's of noble birth, Giselle falls in love with him. When she finds out who he truly is, Giselle realizes she can't marry him, and she goes mad and dies of a weak heart.

This is the story of Eli and me. I'm Giselle and Eli is the lying nobleman. At times, he pretends to be someone he's not. A vulnerable boy who cried on my shoulder. A caring boy who tried to visit me after my surgery. But those versions of Eli aren't real. In truth, he's simply a trickster.

And after a million years of knowing him, I still seem to fall for his tricks.

Chapter 15

Secrets Revealed

TUESDAY

When I wake up, Eli is standing by my side of the bed, staring down at me. His eyebrows are pulled together.

"Were you having a nightmare?" he asks.

I sit up and wipe my eyes. My chest feels clammy. The last thing I remember before waking up is sitting on the studio floor, crying over my snapped ankle. Avery Johnson didn't try to help or ask if I was okay. He looked at me with disdain and said those words again: *You'll never be the dancer you once were.* I really hate that my dreams have turned him into a villain.

"You kept tossing and turning," Eli says. "And then you started making this grunting noise."

"I'm fine." I push the covers away so that I can see my ankle and make sure it's still there in one piece. I want to reach down and touch it, but I won't do that with Eli standing right here. He's still looking at me with concern.

"I'm fine," I repeat.

"We have to check out soon," he says. "We need to decide where we're gonna go."

We should probably drive straight down to North Carolina. That way Eli can go with his dad and I can be alone and mentally prepare for my audition tomorrow.

Tomorrow. It came so fast. Suddenly I feel like I need more time. On cue, my stomach ties itself in knots.

Eli's phone starts ringing. As it vibrates around on the bed, I see that the person calling is Larissa.

"Hey, Riss," he answers. "I'm not with Dad right now. . . . No, I'm not at Mom's either." He pauses. "I'm in D.C., actually."

I stand up and shake out my arms and legs. While Eli talks to Larissa, I walk to the bathroom to brush my teeth. Geezer trots over to me and I bend down to scratch his head. Thanks to him lying between Eli and me, sleeping in the same bed wasn't nearly as awkward as it could have been.

When I finish showering and getting dressed, I walk back into the room to see Eli sitting on the bed with a big smile on his face. When I frown in response, his smile falls, but only a little.

"Larissa said we can stay with her," he says.

Any situation where we don't have to sneak Geezer into another hotel, or where Eli and I don't have to share a bed, is fine with me. Plus, it's not like I have money to stay in another hotel. "Perfect."

We stop at a gas station in Virginia, about a half hour away from St. Maria College where Larissa is enrolled. Our playlist this time is a mix of today's R & B (me) and '90s rap (Eli). Eli is trying to figure out how to work the gas pump, but he's having trouble. He keeps cursing under his breath, and when a man walks over to offer help, Eli grunts and says he's okay. He probably doesn't want people to know we're spoiled kids from New Jersey who've never had to pump our own gas. When he finally gets the pump to work, he sports the world's most satisfied grin.

"Hey," he says, poking his head into the window. "Wanna hear something funny?"

"Your idea of funny and my idea of funny are very different," I say. "So, no."

He continues anyway. "When we were younger, I used to think that Trey liked you. When he told me he was gay a couple months ago, I was like, 'Wait, didn't you like Chloe?'" He laughs. "Funny, right?"

I shrug. "I thought he liked me, too."

"Really?" He leans in farther and raises an eyebrow.

"I kissed him just before he moved. Then he told me he was gay." Now I'm the one laughing. "It was so embarrassing."

I expect Eli to laugh, too, but he just looks confused.

"You kissed Trey," he repeats. "When?"

"I just told you. The summer he moved. We were hanging out at my house one day."

He scratches the back of his neck. "Where was I?"

"I don't know. With your dad, I think."

"Oh." He steps away, fiddles with the gas-pump nozzle, and doesn't say anything else.

I thought for sure he'd love hearing about how I embarrassed myself in front of Trey. Maybe it's only funny to me.

After the tank is filled up, Eli walks around the car and climbs into the driver's seat. We merge back onto the highway, and for a while there's only the sound of LL Cool J saying he needs an around the way girl.

Suddenly, Eli says, "I never knew that you liked Trey."

I look at him in surprise. "I didn't like him. For, like, a second, I thought *he* liked *me*, but I was wrong, obviously. It was stupid. We laughed about it afterward."

He drums his fingers against the steering wheel, and I can tell he's thinking hard about what he's going to say next. "So . . . was that your first kiss?"

"Yes," I say slowly. I shift in my seat to get a better look at him.

He licks his lips, and my eyes fall to his mouth.

WHY AM I STARING AT HIS MOUTH AGAIN?

I turn away and look straight ahead.

A little smugly, he says, "If I were your first kiss, it probably would have been better. Just saying."

Immediately, my cheeks grow hot.

Then he laughs. He's not flirting with me. He's joking,

of course. I force out a laugh, too. *I thought he was flirting with me, but he wasn't! Ha-ha! How hilarious!*

It's a relief when we need to pull over to let Geezer go to the bathroom. As Eli stands with him on the side of the road, I try to get myself together. If I'm not careful, I'll end up just like Giselle. Flirting is just something Eli does. He'd flirt with a tree if it had boobs.

More importantly, it's Eli! Hello! I don't need any reminders as to why I shouldn't care if he's flirting with me or not.

All I need to worry about is my audition.

"Riss just texted and said she can't wait to see you," he says when he gets back in the car.

I avoid looking at him. "I can't wait to see her, either."

Larissa. Now that's a girl who didn't get easily flustered by boys. Before she went away to college, she was the most confident person I knew.

"Everything good?" Eli asks.

"Yep," I say, channeling what I remember of Larissa's cool confidence. "Everything's good."

Chapter 16

Wishes for Daughters

Every year at the Philadelphia Center for Dance, graduating seniors choreograph their own pieces for the spring recital. Larissa's senior year, she choreographed a *pas de deux* for the two of us to perform, and she named the piece "Footsteps." The choreography was a ripple effect. I mimicked each of her movements, so it seemed like I was trying to copy her, but I was really just trying to follow in her footsteps. Female *pas de deux* are rare. I think that's why Larissa wanted us to perform one—she was always somebody who thought outside of the box.

I'd been trying to follow her footsteps in real life, too. Larissa felt like the older sister I never had. She always came to the mall with Mom and me to help pick out my school clothes, and she did my makeup before our shows. I was at the dance studio when I got my period for the first time, and Larissa was the one who explained how to use a tampon.

We were the only Black girls at our studio, and I'd joined because Ms. Linda suggested that Mom put me in ballet to keep me busy. It was just after my dad had died, and Mom was still getting used to being a single parent to a three-year-old. The memory of sitting beside Larissa in the back seat of Ms. Linda's car, wearing pink tights and black leotards, is still so clear in my mind.

I wanted to be just like her: beautiful and confident. She was one of the best dancers in the senior company, but she'd already made up her mind to quit ballet after graduation, much to Ms. Linda's disappointment. She'd be starting college in Virginia at the end of summer, leaving dance behind. And me.

The audience applauded when we finished our piece. Someone even whistled. The praise continued when we hurried offstage into the wings and our classmates congratulated us. I felt too many things: happiness that we danced well and sadness that this was the last time we'd dance together. I looked up at Larissa's smiling face and surprised even myself when I started to cry.

Our recitals were always held at the local middle school, so Larissa knew where to go when she quickly ushered me to the bathroom. She closed the door and checked the stalls to make sure we were alone.

"What's wrong?" she asked, wetting a paper towel and using it to wipe my smudged mascara.

"What am I going to do when you leave?" I blubbered.

"Who's going to help me with my makeup? You're the only one who looks like me. I'll be all alone."

"You'll be okay." She hugged me close. "I promise you'll be okay."

"No, I won't," I said. "You're going to forget about me once you start college."

She pulled back and looked at me. Fiercely, she said, "I would never do that. And you are strong enough to be on your own." She softened her voice. "You're meant for this, Chloe. Dancing is in your heart. With or without me, you'll continue to be great. I was never really meant for this. It's just something I happened to be good at, but it doesn't make me happy."

I looked at our reflections in the bathroom mirror. We wore matching long-sleeve black leotards and black tights. Maybe someone could have confused us for real sisters. My cheeks were blotchy and wet from crying, while Larissa's face looked fresh and relaxed. She took the bobby pins out of her hair and undid her bun. Her thick hair sprang free and she scratched her scalp, watching me with a small smile.

"You're going to keep getting better and better," she said. "One of these days I'm gonna have to buy tickets to see you on tour with the New York City Ballet or something."

"Maybe." I felt myself begin to smile.

"Virginia is far, but you know how bad I need to get away from my mom," she said. "You can always come visit me. Remember that."

I nodded, and she put her arm around me as we walked to the designated "backstage" classroom. Mom and Ms. Linda were already waiting for us.

"Oh, what happened to the beautiful bun I did for you this morning, Larissa?" Ms. Linda asked, taking in her daughter's wild hair. "Couldn't you have waited until we got home to take it out?"

"No," Larissa said simply. She took off her pointe shoes, tossed them into her dance bag, and slid on her sneakers. "Can we go now, please?"

Ms. Linda frowned. "But don't you want to stay and watch the rest of the recital?"

"Not really, no."

"Well, all right, I guess." Ms. Linda walked over and hugged me. "You danced so beautifully, Miss Thing. You keep on dancing, you hear? It breaks my heart that Larissa is giving it all up so easily." She looked at Mom. "She *still* doesn't know what she wants to major in. I don't see why she can't at least be a dance minor."

Larissa sighed. "Mom, please."

Ms. Linda turned to her. "What? I'm just saying."

Larissa closed her eyes and took a deep breath. "Okay, Mom."

"Who do you think you're rolling your eyes at?" Ms. Linda snapped.

"Linda," Mom said, stepping in. "Let's save this conversation for another time." She gestured to the rest of the dancers and their parents in the room. More quietly, she added, "Let's not make a scene."

Ms. Linda pursed her lips and nodded.

Larissa hugged me one more time before they left. I wanted to go with her, but I still had two more performances, so I stayed backstage and Mom helped me change into my next costume.

Later that night as we drove home from the recital, Mom cleared her throat and then turned down the radio. I knew it meant she wanted to talk.

"It's sad that Larissa gives her mother such a hard time," she said. "If Linda thinks Larissa should give minoring in dance a try, then that's what Larissa should do."

I thought of how sure Larissa was about her decision to leave dance behind. It seemed unfair that Ms. Linda was bitter over a choice Larissa had made in order to be happy.

So I asked, "But shouldn't Larissa do what makes her happy?"

Mom sighed. "She's young. She doesn't know what's best for her." We reached a red light and she turned to me. "That's what parents are for. We point you in the right direction until you're ready to make your own decisions. That's what I want you to know."

I had a feeling that what Mom said wasn't completely true.

Chapter 17

It Starts Here

We reach St. Maria in the afternoon. Eli comes to visit Larissa at least twice a year, so he navigates easily through the campus neighborhood and knows where to park. As we walk to Larissa's dorm, we pass old brick buildings and students wearing red St. Maria sweatshirts and hats. They walk briskly, gripping the straps of their book bags. When we reach her dorm, a group of boys are throwing a football back and forth, and Eli has to hold tight on to Geezer's leash so he doesn't take off after the ball and ruin their game.

Larissa emerges from her building and I stare at her in shock. Her thick, curly hair is gone. She's now sporting a slicked-down pixie cut. And she's wearing baggy denim overalls with rips in the knees. Her face used to be glamorously made up every day, and now it's bare.

She jogs toward us, and the bright smile on her face dims as she gets closer. She hugs Eli, but she quickly pulls away, frowning. "Why didn't you tell me you were bringing the dog?"

"I did tell you," he says.

"No, you didn't. I would have remembered." She puts her hands on her hips. "Especially since we can't have animals in the dorm! Eli, what am I supposed to do with him?"

"You can sneak him in," he suggests. "We did that at our hotel last night. It was difficult, but doable."

She sighs and turns her attention to me. "You're finally here!" she says. Her embrace is warm and secure. I take a step back and marvel again at how different she looks.

"Larissa," I say. "Your *hair*."

She pats her scalp. "What about it?"

"It's . . . it's all gone!"

"Oh." She laughs; it's loud and unguarded. "I cut it forever ago during sophomore year. It's been so long since we last saw each other."

I nod dumbly. "It has."

"But who cares about me? You are *gorgeous*, Chloe." She grins, and it reminds me of Eli.

My cheeks heat up, and I shake my head.

"Yes, you are. Just look at you!" She grabs my arm and twirls me in a circle. Eli starts to laugh.

"Look at her," Larissa says to him, delighted. "Isn't she absolutely gorgeous?"

Eli stops laughing. He turns away and clears his throat. "Can you let us inside, Riss? I need a nap."

"I'm serious about the dog. I can't bring him inside." She pulls out her phone and starts texting quickly. "Maybe Will won't mind if you bring him over there."

Eli smirks. "Of course he won't. He's trying to score brownie points with his girlfriend's little brother."

"Be nice, Elijah," Larissa says, smiling at her phone. "Will said it's fine for you to bring Geezer there. You remember the way to his house, right? I'd go with you, but I have class in a few minutes and I don't want to be late."

Eli frowns. "I didn't know you had class right now. Why didn't you say something when I called?"

"Probably because I was half asleep! I'm sorry. I wasn't thinking about it at the time. I thought you guys could just chill in my room until I got back. I didn't know you had the dog."

"But your only brother in the world is here," he says. "Can't you skip?"

"No, it's one of my favorite classes and we're prepping for an exam."

"I pass exams that I don't prep for all the time."

Larissa shakes her head. "Yeah, *high school* exams. Anyway, it will be nice for you to spend some time with Will for a little bit. You'll get to hang out with me soon, I promise."

"Fine," Eli huffs, throwing his duffel bag over his shoulder. He looks at me. "Ready?"

Before I can answer, Larissa links her arm through mine. "Wait, Chloe, you should definitely sit in on this class with me. It's called Femininity, Beauty, and the Black Female Body, but we say FBBFB for short."

I look between the two of them. To go with Eli or to stay with Larissa?

Duh, I'm going to choose to stay with her over being stuck with him.

"I'll stay with you," I say.

Eli nods like he figured that's what I would say. "Have fun with BFFF."

"It's *FBBFB*," Larissa corrects him.

"That's what I meant," he calls over his shoulder as he walks away, steering Geezer down the sidewalk.

Larissa shakes her head and watches him with a faint smile on her face. She turns to me. "All right, let's go."

❧

First, she takes me inside her dorm so she can grab her books. The dorm is co-ed, but she lives on an all-girls floor. Someone is blasting Kehlani, and there's a constant rising and falling of voices and laughter.

She opens her room door and motions to her side of the room so that I can put down my bag. Her side is organized and simple, and her comforter set is plain and cream-colored. Beside a neat stack of books, there's a framed photograph of her and Eli on her desk, and a pair of black Doc Martens and white Stan Smiths sit by the foot of her bed.

Her roommate's side of the room has a little bit more going on. There's a pile of colorful clothes on her bed and over a dozen posters of dancers on her wall: salsa dancers spinning and break-dancers frozen in position. My stomach tightens, remembering the way I was too afraid to volunteer for the street performance in D.C.

"Is your roommate a dancer?" I ask.

"Yeah, that's Wei," Larissa says. "You'll probably meet her later."

We head to her class, and the campus feels so alive. Everywhere I turn, there's something happening. A club holding a bake sale, or groups of friends sitting on the lawn, laughing and listening to music, or students passing out flyers for upcoming events. A lot of people say hello to Larissa. It's not surprising. She was popular in high school, too.

Larissa introduces me to her FBBFB professor, Dr. Booth, a tall woman with dark brown skin who wears a bright orange dress with a matching head wrap. Larissa tells her that I'm a student from her old high school and that I'm spending my spring break visiting colleges. Dr. Booth eagerly agrees to let me sit in on the class and explains that FBBFB analyzes how Black women have been depicted in media over the last fifty years. Once we sit down, she quickly launches into a discussion about the angry Black woman stereotype on reality television.

Larissa hands me some notebook paper and a pen, and

she spends the rest of the class vigorously taking notes and raising her hand to ask questions. She gets into a heated debate with a classmate over whether or not reality stars should come clean about what drama is scripted and what drama is real on their shows, and by the time class ends, she's practically glowing. In all the years I've known and danced with her, I've never seen her look this happy.

On our way back to her dorm, we stop at a campus café so she can get coffee, and she buys me a chocolate cupcake from the bake sale. As we walk, she explains what she loves about dual-majoring in Africana Studies and Women's Studies.

I'm listening, but I'm also paying attention to everything that's happening around me. I realize this is the life I could have, the life Mom probably wants for me. I could walk through a beautiful campus every day, take cool classes, and maybe major in dance and minor in whatever I find interesting.

But even as I think this, I know I could never be as happy as Larissa is here.

"Do you ever miss it?" I ask, interrupting her.

She raises an eyebrow. "Miss what?"

"Dancing," I say. "Ballet."

"Sometimes." She smiles a little. "My mom's still low-key mad that I quit. But now she has a long list of other things that make her mad. My hair is short. She thinks I dress like a little boy. She doesn't think my majors will lead to a good

146

job. Let's just say I'm definitely not looking forward to being at her house for Easter."

"But you're happy," I say.

Her smile grows. "Yeah. I'm really happy."

"At least Eli will be going to UNC and eventually to law school like your dad," I offer. "Your mom can be happy about that."

She blinks. Slowly, she says, "Yeah . . . I guess that's true." She tosses her coffee cup in the trash and puts her arm around me. "So, speaking of Eli, he told me all about your audition. Avery Johnson, huh? He's so amazing." She gives my shoulders a little squeeze. "Are you ready?"

"No," I say honestly. "I thought I was at first, but now I don't think I am. I haven't felt the same about my dancing since my accident."

"Don't doubt yourself, Chloe."

"You're the second person this week who's told me to stop doubting myself, but *how* do I do that? You've always been confident. It's easier for you to say."

"Confidence starts here," she says, pointing at my heart. "You have to take hold of the world and demand that it gives you what you want. That's what I do. It doesn't always come easy, regardless of how it looks. *You* are already doing it now by choosing to go to your audition."

"I never thought of it that way," I say.

"It sounds like you need to give yourself a little more credit." She looks at me closely. "Sometimes people might believe in themselves, but it's not enough when they feel like they don't have support. How does your mom feel about you auditioning?"

"She doesn't know," I say. "She's on vacation."

Larissa starts to laugh, almost as uncontrollably as Eli did last night when I started barking on the phone. After she catches her breath, she says, "I knew it! I just knew it. When Eli told me you were with him, I thought to myself, there is no way Ms. Carol let her daughter travel all the way to Virginia with my brother."

"I don't like that I had to lie to her," I say, feeling the guilt rise up.

"I know, but you've gotta do what you've gotta do, right?" She shrugs. "But, like I said, it starts here." She puts her hand over her heart. "Now you say it."

I stare at her. "Say what?"

"'It starts here,'" she repeats. "Come on, say it."

I sigh. Weakly, I say, "It starts here." I feel silly.

"That was *terrible.* Say it again. With feeling this time."

"It starts here," I repeat, tapping my chest.

"Louder!"

"It starts here!"

"Louder!" she shouts again.

"It starts here!" I pound my chest. "It starts here!"

People walk by and stare at us. But I don't care because shouting like this really does help.

Larissa smiles. "That was good. Sometimes we need to just shout it out, you know?"

"I really wish I could just sneak into somebody's dance studio for an hour," I say. "I need to get in the right mind-set."

"I think I might have a solution for that." She grabs my hand. "Come on."

Chapter 18

Dance Is Art

Larissa takes me back to her room so I can get my bag and change into my dance clothes. We hurry across campus and then stop in front of another building. Students carrying instruments are milling on the steps.

"This is the performing arts building," Larissa explains as we head for the door.

Inside, I hear the sound of someone playing the piano coming from one end of the hall. Larissa leads me downstairs to the basement, where the dance studios are. I get jittery as we pass each one, glancing in at what looks like a jazz class.

When we reach the end of the hall, Larissa pauses. Reggae is playing on the other side of the door.

"I'm pretty sure they still practice here," she says. She quietly opens the door and peeks her head in. "Hi, ladies!"

Someone shouts, "Riss!"

Larissa pushes the door wider to reveal two girls standing in the middle of the studio wearing sneakers and sweats.

One girl is tall and lithe; her shiny, dark hair is cut into a blunt bob.

The other girl is short and curvy, with long braids that fall to the middle of her back. She walks over to the speaker and cuts off the music. "And to what do we owe this visit?" she asks.

"I want to introduce you to someone," Larissa says, gesturing to me. "This is my friend Chloe Pierce, from back home." She nods at the girl with the bob cut. "Chloe, this is my roommate, Wei Chen, and this is our friend, Sinead Harper."

Sinead smiles wide and friendly. "You can call me Sin for short. That's what everybody calls me, for obvious reasons."

Wei rolls her eyes and steps forward to shake my hand. "No one calls her that."

"I need a favor," Larissa says. "Chloe has an audition tomorrow and she needs somewhere to practice. Can she use this room, pretty please?"

"Of course," Wei says. "We were mostly just messing around, anyway."

Wistfully, Sinead says, "I thought you might be here because you wanted to rejoin the dance team."

"Rejoin?" I repeat, looking at Larissa.

She smiles a little sheepishly. "I was on the team for a couple months—"

"More like a couple weeks," Sinead interjects.

"—freshman year, because I wanted to see if a different style of dance might be more fun. Turns out I just needed a complete break." She points at me. "Don't tell my mom. I'd never hear the end of it."

I cross my heart. "Promise not to."

Larissa says she'll be back in an hour or so, and the girls leave the room to me. As soon as the door shuts behind them, the jitters take over my body again. Energy courses through my veins, because my body knows that it's finally about to dance.

The first thing I do is hook up my phone to the stereo system. At the Philadelphia Center for Dance, there's a pianist who plays classical music during class. But whenever I dance alone, I listen to my own playlists. "Nothing Even Matters" by Lauryn Hill and D'Angelo begins to play.

I sit down in front of the mirrors that span the entire wall. I take off my Chucks and point and flex my toes. They're rough and calloused, and my toenails have to be kept short for my pointe shoes. Right now I have a particularly nasty blister on my big toe that's finally starting to heal since I haven't danced in a few days. It takes hard and ugly work to make ballet look beautiful.

I wrap my toes with tape and put on my toe pads before I slide my feet into my pointe shoes, wrapping the ribbons around my ankles and tying them with secure knots. I always take longer when wrapping my left ankle so that the ribbons do a better job at covering my scar.

I stand up and shake out my legs and stretch my arms. I place my hand on the barre and breathe deeply. Ballet is as mental as it is physical. It's not enough to just hold your center and move gracefully, weightless like a feather. You have to *be* that feather and visualize the center of your body remaining poised and firm, floating through the air.

At the barre, I square my hips and elongate my neck, and begin with *demi-pliés*, bending my knees in first position, then second, third, fourth, and fifth. I move on to *grand pliés*, *tendus*, and *dégagés*, before I rise up on my toes and balance in *soutenu* for as long as I can. Then I work on combinations across the floor. My favorite is *tombé, pas de bourrée, glissade, jeté*. It looks like I'm gingerly stepping and brushing my way into a leap, but it's a lot more work than that, of course.

After my surgery, I'd expected everything to come back to me easily. Sometimes that was the case and sometimes it wasn't. What I didn't expect was the intense anger and disappointment I felt when I faltered and missed a simple step. Those were the days that I danced harder and came home with bigger blisters and bloodier toes.

I'm tired of the doubt riding on my shoulders every day like a heavy creature, and I'm tired of the nightmares. I know what I have to do. I stand in the middle of the floor and close my eyes, pretending to be Odile, the black swan in *Swan Lake* who tricks Prince Siegfried into believing that she is the white swan, his true love. Odile does thirty-two *fouettés*. She is not the type of girl who would doubt herself.

I prep and start whipping around, using the reflection of the stereo in the mirror to spot. I ignore the sound from my dream of my ankle bone cracking and push myself to keep turning. But then Avery Johnson's face pops into my head, saying I'll never be the dancer I once was, and it's not easy to ignore. I come out of the turn and catch my balance before I fall. I shake out my legs again and pause, trying to catch my breath.

Thirteen *fouettés*. It's way more than I've done in my nightmares, but less than how many I've done before in real life.

Sometimes people might believe in themselves, but it's not enough when they feel like they don't have support.

It's interesting that Larissa followed that statement with asking about Mom. Ballet is the only thing that makes me feel completely free, and now she's trying to keep me away from it and I don't understand why. Other than my accident, I've never given her any reason to believe that I wouldn't be able to take care of myself. But I'm finally deciding that I can't carry around any more doubt, hers or mine.

I prep again and begin turning. *I can do this*, I repeat every time I spot my reflection in the mirror as I spin. When I make it past thirteen, I turn faster with a new rush of energy. With each turn, it feels like I'm letting go of anything and everything that's been holding me back. When I make it to twenty, I finally stumble out. It's not thirty-two, but I stand in the middle of the room in awe. Twenty is more than I've done in months.

I walk back to the barre and steady myself against it. My face is sweaty, my cheeks are flushed, and my bun is sloppy. I look and feel unraveled. But not in a bad way. I feel weightless.

I catch a movement in the corner of the room, and I turn around to find Eli standing at the door, watching me.

"How long have you been there?" I ask.

"Not that long." He steps into the studio, and I notice he's holding his sketchbook. "I was looking for you. Riss said you'd be here."

"Oh," is all I can think to say.

"Did you miss me?" he asks.

I can't help but roll my eyes. "Not really."

He smirks and walks farther into the room. Sunlight peeks through the top of the basement windows and shines onto his face. "It's wild how you do all those turns. I lost count after a while. Is it hard?"

"It is at first."

I lean back against the barre, and he walks to the opposite end of the studio. Now we're staring at each other across the room. I look down at my pointe shoes, acutely aware of how sweaty I am.

"Where's Geezer?" I ask.

"At Will's house. I wanted to bring him, but there's too many people on campus. He'd get agitated."

"Oh." I clear my throat. "Well, I'm kind of busy in here, so . . ."

"Can I draw you?"

I blink. "What?"

"Can I draw you?" he repeats, easing himself down so that he's sitting on the floor pretzel-style. He opens his sketchbook to a clean page.

"You mean you want me to pose, like for a portrait?"

"No. I'll draw you while you dance."

"I don't think so. You'll distract me."

"I'll be really quiet. You'll forget I'm even here."

I shake my head. "I doubt that."

"Please?" he says. "I promise to show you once I'm done."

This is enough to make me change my mind. "Okay."

The song changes to "I Wanna Be Where You Are" by the Jackson 5, and I step back into the center of the floor to work on more combinations. Even though I'm wearing a leotard and tights, I feel exposed. I can't remember the last time Eli saw me dance. Most likely some time in middle school when there was a stage and an audience between us. Never alone like this.

I picture Avery Johnson, because wherever he is, is where *I* want to be. Whether it's auditioning for him, learning at his conservatory, or, if I'm lucky, being a professional dancer with his company.

But Avery Johnson isn't all I'm thinking about. I can't

stop glancing at Eli's reflection in the mirror. He's skillfully sketching across the page, and every once in a while, I catch him watching me intently.

He said he was looking for me. He came here because he chose to be wherever I was.

Oh, God. Do I even hear myself right now? Why am I reading so deeply into this? He most likely came here because he was bored. That's all.

When my limbs feel gooey and loose and my toes start cramping, I decide that's enough dancing. If I keep going, I might put too much stress on my muscles, and I can't afford to get hurt again.

After I finish my cool-down stretch, I turn around to face Eli. He's staring again. Then he blinks like he's rousing from a dream. I walk over, plop down in front of him, and begin untying my pointe shoes. I'm anxious to see how I appear to him on the page. Will it look like the sketch he gave me before? When I lean over to peek at what he's done, he quickly closes his sketchbook.

"But you promised you'd show me," I say, disappointed. Tricked once again.

"I said I'd show you when I was finished. I'm not finished."

"I really want to see it."

"You will," he says. "I promise."

I nod at his sketchbook. "What else do you have in there?"

I expect him to tell me to mind my business. Instead he looks at me skeptically. "Why do you wanna know?"

"I want to steal your work and sell it. Duh." I roll my eyes. "I'm just curious. If you don't want to show me, it's fine."

Slowly—and surprisingly—he reopens his sketchbook. He slides closer so that one side of the book is in his lap and the other side is in mine. I blink in disbelief. Is this really happening?

"I drew this one earlier," he says. The first drawing is of Geezer lying down, chewing on a deflated basketball. It looks so real. He drew the faint scars on Geezer's muzzle, and the way his right eye is a little smaller than his left.

He flips closer to the front of the sketchbook and reveals a drawing of Larissa. One half of her face has lipstick, big hair, and long, curled eyelashes. Her mouth is turned up in a smile. The other half has short hair, a round, questioning eye, and full lips set in a straight line. Larissa then vs. Larissa now.

I run my fingers over the page. "This is amazing, Eli."

"Thanks," he says. "I'm supposed to tell a story through art for my senior project. I'm just not sure what story I should tell yet."

He keeps turning the pages. He shows me more drawings of his mom and Larissa. There are some of his old basketball teammates and a few of Isiah. A lot of pages are devoted to random sketches of Geezer. The last sketch he shows me is of him and his dad on a fishing boat. Eli looks a lot younger and the expression on his face is sad, even though his dad is smiling. Mr. Greene used to take him on fishing trips all the time when we were younger. But, from this drawing, it doesn't seem like Eli enjoyed this particular trip very much.

I never would have guessed in a million years that he'd show me his art like this. He has such a gift. It would be a shame if he wasted it.

"Why aren't you going to art school?" I ask.

He closes his sketchbook. "I am."

"What?"

"I am going to art school."

I lean forward to get a better look at him. "But I thought you were going to UNC?"

"No."

"But your mom said—"

"My mom saw my UNC acceptance letter and called my dad to tell him the news. They both assumed that's where I was going because that's where he went to college. Neither of them bothered to ask me."

"And you haven't bothered to tell them?"

"You think my dad would be excited to hear that I'm going to college for art? He just wants me to become a lawyer like him. My mom will go along with whatever he says as long as he keeps sending her alimony checks."

"Who else knows?" I ask.

"Larissa and Trey," he says. "And now you."

Well, that explains the weird looks Trey and Larissa gave me whenever I mentioned Eli and UNC. And why Trey said Eli was going through some things.

"Which art school is it?" I ask.

"The San Francisco Art Institute."

"*San Francisco?* Wow, Eli. That's awesome."

"Yeah." He shrugs a little, like it isn't a big deal, but it is.

"When are you going to tell your parents? You have to eventually."

He clears his throat. "Well, I planned on telling my dad this week."

Him putting off arriving at his dad's makes sense now. Even though he won't admit it, I can tell he's nervous.

I think about the time Mom told me that parents push their kids in the right direction until their kids can figure out what they want on their own. But our parents really underestimated us.

"If everything works out the way we want, we'll both be on opposite sides of the country in the fall," he says. "I bet you'll be happy to be far away from me."

I feel the tiniest of pangs in my stomach when he says this, but I ignore it. "The day you move will be the best day of my life. Maybe I'll send you a postcard once I'm in New York."

He smirks. "Who says I'm going to give you my address?"

I start to shove him, but he catches my arm by the elbow. "Why must you be so violent?"

I wait for him to let go, but he doesn't. Instead, he slowly runs his hand down my arm and gently skims his fingers over the scar I got from his thornbush all those years ago. Then he lifts his eyes to meet mine.

My heart is thudding so loudly in my ears I can't hear anything else.

"I'm back."

Eli and I jump apart like we've been zapped.

Larissa is standing at the door, smiling. Her eyes dart back and forth between us. Who knows how long she's been there.

"Ready to get some food?" she asks. "Will said he'd cook."

"Yes," we both answer.

Eli quickly hops up and helps me to my feet. His palm is warm, and his fingers are covered in pencil lead. When he lets go of my hand, I try to shake off the ridiculous feeling that I wish he hadn't.

Chapter 19

Starting Over

Will is a senior, and he lives in a house off campus with a few other upperclassmen. His front door is unlocked, and when Larissa pushes it open, Geezer runs to us. I get a view of the mismatched living-room furniture, and sprawled out on the cracked leather couch is a guy who is string-bean skinny with his hair cut in a fade. He jumps up once he sees us.

Larissa can't finish saying, "Chloe, this is my boyfriend, Will," before he scoops her up into his arms.

"I missed you," he says, nuzzling his nose into the crook of her neck.

"I just saw you this morning." Larissa tries to squirm away, but he holds her closer. She finally stops wiggling and sighs. "Okay. Okay. I missed you, too."

Eli makes a gagging noise, but they ignore him as Will gently sets her down and brushes a hand over her short hair. He smiles at Larissa like she's perfect, and then he turns to look at me. He picks up my hand and gives it a firm shake.

"Nice to meet you. I hope you like ramen noodles from the pack, because that's all I know how to cook."

"That's fine," I say, laughing. I point at the Greek letters on his T-shirt. "What does that say?"

He puffs up his chest. "Beta Beta Beta. It's a biological-science honor society. Sometimes people think I'm in a frat, which is hilarious. Because, no."

He leads us into the kitchen, where a pot of ramen noodles is boiling on the stove. His roommates come in and out, grabbing food from the fridge and introducing themselves briefly before they scurry away.

"They're playing video games in the basement," Larissa explains to me. She nods at Will. "He'd be right with them if I weren't here."

"I heard that," Will says. He walks over and places mismatched bowls filled with noodles on the table.

Eli's hand knocks into mine as we both reach for the same bowl. I quickly pull away, remembering how strange I felt earlier when he grabbed my hand in the dance studio.

"Go ahead," I say. "You can have that one."

"No, you can have it," he says.

Larissa reaches for the bowl and quirks an eyebrow. "How about I take it?"

Will sits down, and we start to eat. Eli is feeding Geezer some of his noodles when Larissa asks him to take his hat off at the table.

Eli snorts. "Okay, Mom."

"I'm serious, Eli," Larissa says. "Come on."

"I'm serious, too," he says. "I'm not taking it off."

She squints at him. Slowly, she asks, "What's wrong with your hair? You love any opportunity to show off those curls of yours." She glances at me and my face must give something away, because Larissa pushes back her chair and stands.

"Stop, Riss," Eli says. He gets up and walks around the table to get away from her. Geezer trails after him like they're playing a game of follow-the-leader.

"Not until you show me what you're hiding under that hat."

Eli breaks out into a full-on run and Larissa chases him. He jumps onto the living-room couch and holds out his arm to keep her at bay. "Don't touch me. I'm serious."

Larissa the ballerina makes a reappearance as she gracefully sidesteps his extended arm and swipes his hat off of his head, revealing his bald spot for all of us to see.

"Oh shit," Will says.

Larissa's jaw drops, and I cover my mouth to keep from laughing.

Eli clears his throat. "So . . . what had happened was—"

"I don't even want to know what happened," Larissa says. "You're going to have to cut all of your hair so it grows back evenly. You know that, right?"

He balks at this. "No."

"Yes," she says. "Chloe, please tell him I'm right."

"She's right," I say, still trying not to laugh. Eli glares at me.

"Your hair grows fast," Larissa says. "The curls will be back before you know it."

He shakes his head. "I'd rather have a bald spot than be bald! Everyone will call me Mr. Clean."

"Or an old man," I say.

"Or an old man!" Eli yells.

Larissa gives me a look that lets me know I'm not helping.

"What are you going to do at school?" she asks. "Be reasonable. You have to let Will cut it."

"Me?" Will says, blinking.

Slowly, Eli lowers his hands from his head. He sighs and looks down at the floor. "Fine." His gaze snaps back up to Larissa and then to Will. "Please don't make me look stupid."

After we finish eating, we move outside onto Will's back porch so he can cut Eli's hair. Eli mopes in his chair as he watches clumps fall to the floor by his feet. Geezer sniffs at them, sneezing every few seconds.

Larissa and I sit at the bottom of the porch steps. She hums along to the music playing on her phone, totally relaxed. Meanwhile, I keep thinking about how every minute that ticks by brings me closer to my audition. Dancing in the studio earlier helped, and this is the most I've had my nerves under control all week, but I would be lying if I said my stomach wasn't doing flips.

The song changes, and Larissa suddenly stands up and holds out her hand.

"Dance with me, for old times' sake," she says.

Smiling, I let her pull me up, and I follow her lead as she dances the same choreography from our *pas de deux*. When she begins to stumble over the steps, I take the lead instead and she follows. Then she stops dancing and watches me, smiling proudly.

"You really are meant for this," she says.

Our moment is interrupted when Will shouts, "Behold, my masterpiece!"

He holds a mirror in front of Eli, who raises an eyebrow like he's unsure what to make of his new look. He's not completely bald. Will left a bit of peach fuzz. The haircut makes him look older and more sophisticated. I feel a flutter in my stomach the longer I look at him.

"Thoughts?" Will asks, surveying his work.

Eli shrugs, turning his head this way and that to get a better look. "It's not bad."

"It's definitely much better than having a bald spot," Larissa says.

Eli's eyes find mine. "What do you think?"

It's an ironic question, because without thinking, I blurt, "You look handsome."

ME AND MY MOUTH.

Eli flashes a small smile and thanks me. I'm busy wishing the ground would open up and swallow me whole.

My state of mortification thankfully ends when the song changes and Will tells Larissa it's his turn to dance with her. He makes his way toward her and puts his hands around her waist. They sway slowly to the music and gaze at each other.

I make a move to sit on the porch, but I hesitate. I don't want to sit next to Eli after the compliment I just gave him.

But wouldn't I look weird if I *didn't* sit next to him? I just need to be cool.

As I approach, Eli slides over to make room for me. When I sit down, Geezer lies in front of us, and we watch as Larissa and Will sway back and forth.

"It's nice to see them together," Eli says. "It's like proof that we don't have to have dysfunctional relationships just because our parents had one."

I nod, facing forward. I still can't bring myself to look at him.

"That school has to accept you," he says. "You're amazing—I mean your dancing. Your dancing is amazing."

Surprised, I finally turn to look at him. Pink spots blossom on both of his cheeks. I don't know what surprises me more: his compliment or the fact that he's blushing.

But I'm blushing, too. I'm sure of it. "Thank you."

"You're welcome."

That might be the nicest thing he's ever said to me. I'm still marveling over it when he breaks the silence again.

"When I was watching you dance earlier, I kept thinking

that I was witnessing some kind of miracle," he says. "You broke your ankle, but there you were, dancing like you'd never been injured in the first place." He shifts so that he's facing me head-on. "What you said yesterday was right. I wasn't the one who almost hit you, but if I'd driven you to the dance like I'd said I would, you probably wouldn't have gotten hurt. I know that. I think I've always known that."

I stare at him. I've waited months to hear him say those words and staring is all I can do.

"I knew I should've apologized, but I didn't know how," he continues. "I spent a long time thinking it over, and when I finally knew what I wanted to say, it felt like it was too late." He looks down and traces his foot over a crack in the porch. "I wasn't purposely ignoring you at school, either. Sometimes I'd see you in the hallway, and I'd want to apologize right there, but I was afraid you'd yell at me in front of everyone."

"I might've," I admit. He looks up and smirks.

"Anyway, what I'm trying to say is that what I did was messed up. You deserved better. I'm sorry, and I hope you can forgive me."

I'm quiet as I let his words sink in.

Part of me wants to be the kind of girl who would make someone beg for her forgiveness, who has the ability to watch someone squirm. I shouldn't forgive him so easily, should I?

But I'm tired of holding on to this grudge. I want so badly for us to start over.

"Yeah," I finally say. "I forgive you."

His smile is full of relief and gratitude. "How you feeling about tomorrow? Nervous?"

"A little," I say, as the jitters return. "I love ballet more than anything, but I have to admit it's been nice to get a break from it these past few days."

"You'll be all right," he says.

He gives my hand a reassuring squeeze, and leaves his hand placed over mine. It almost looks like our fingers are entwined. I keep waiting for him to pull away, but he doesn't. When I look up at his face, he's already looking at me. His expression is serious, a little unreadable. Have his eyes always been so brown? They're the color of milk chocolate. I've known him my whole life. Why haven't I noticed this before?

"You should come with me to my dad's house after your audition instead of driving home," he says. "He lives on the beach, and he has a huge TV, so you can watch any movie you want. Even *Forrest Gump*."

The corner of his mouth twitches. Slowly, his lips form into a smile. It's infectious. I can't help but smile in return as I fumble to come up with a reply to his offer.

And that's how Larissa finds us, smiling at each other and almost holding hands. Somehow, she and Will stopped dancing and turned off the music, and I didn't even notice.

"I have an eight a.m. class," she says to me. "I'm gonna head back now. Ready to go?"

"Yes." I stand up quickly and try to ignore my tingling hand.

Larissa gives Eli a quick forehead peck and tells him she'll see him tomorrow.

"Bye, Chlo," Eli says.

He smiles at me. It isn't his wolfish smile. This one is open and genuine, almost innocent. It's a smile that will be stuck in my head.

"Bye, Eli."

$$\sim\!\!\!\mathcal{J}\!\!\!\sim$$

I avoid looking at Larissa on the walk back to her dorm. I have a feeling she's going to ask me about her brother.

"I'm so happy the two of you made up," she finally says.

"Me and Eli?" I don't know why I say that, because of course she means us.

"He was so upset after your accident. You would've thought somebody displayed all of his artwork for the world to see, and you know how he gets when people look at his art without permission."

She stops walking and puts her hand on my shoulder to stop me, too.

"He's a good kid, right?" she asks. "I know he can be difficult sometimes, and it's hard to understand why he acts the way he does, but underneath it all he's not so bad, is he?"

She looks worried. Almost like a mom asking a schoolteacher about her child's behavior in class.

"No," I say, and I find that I really mean it. "He's not so bad."

Chapter 20

Audition Day

WEDNESDAY

I barely slept last night. I was too excited and nervous. In the early morning hours when I finally drifted off and eased into that space between asleep and awake, I imagined that I was in the audition studio building. I walked through the hall, wearing my homecoming dress and shoes, and even though this was out of the ordinary, I wasn't alarmed. Somehow, I felt like I would be okay. But when I rounded the corner, I saw Mom. She stood with her arms crossed, blocking the studio door, disappointment etched into her features.

I froze, torn between asking for forgiveness and begging her to move. She opened her mouth, and I waited for her to berate me, to tell me all the ways in which I was a lying and untrustworthy daughter. But, instead, the noise she made sounded like an alarm clock.

"I hate eight a.m. classes," Larissa grumbles, stopping the alarm on her phone.

It's 7:30 a.m. I'm curled up in a sleeping bag on Larissa's

dorm room floor. Wei is snoring, and Larissa is groggily getting out of bed. This is where I am, not in a hallway about to be confronted by Mom.

This is reality. It's audition day.

~❦~

Larissa walks me outside, where Eli and Geezer are waiting. She gives me a long hug good-bye.

"You'll be perfect," she whispers in my ear. "Let me know how it goes, okay?"

I nod, wondering if she can feel how clammy my palms are.

I'm trying to stay in the present and focus, but my thoughts are all over the place. That dream with Mom really spooked me. What would she say if she knew what I was doing right now? And my thoughts are on Avery Johnson, too. What will he be like in person? How good will the other dancers be?

Eli and Larissa say their good-byes, and I step back to give them privacy. They hug, and when she pulls away, she holds her hands on either side of his face. She speaks to him in a whisper, and Eli listens, nodding intently.

"See you at Easter!" Larissa yells as we head for the parking lot.

I'd like to bring her with me, but I know I'll be okay without her, too. I wave until she turns around and jogs away to class.

When we're back on the road, Eli fidgets with his phone, trying to hook it up to the aux cord and drive at the same time.

"Give me that," I say. "You're going to get us into another accident."

"Sorry." He smirks and drops his phone into my lap.

I'm not sure how to act around him since yesterday. I forgave him, and I really meant it, but now where do we stand? Are we friends? Maybe. But then why did I feel strange whenever he touched me yesterday? Why did I stay up late last night, wondering what I should have said when he invited me to his dad's house? I don't have to go home right after the audition, and now I might not want to. I just wish I knew if he really meant it. He hasn't brought it up again yet.

This is bad timing. I can't wonder about Eli *and* try to focus on my audition.

"Hello, what's going on over there, DJ?" he asks.

Right. I'm supposed to be picking a song to play. I scroll through his music library but none of his songs feel right, and I can't find a song to play on my phone either. Nothing speaks to the mood I'm in: overwhelmed.

"Is it okay if we don't listen to anything?" I ask.

He glances at me. "Yeah, that's cool."

I close my eyes and try to remind myself of how calm I felt while dancing in the studio yesterday. But that makes me think about how Eli interrupted me. And once again, how it felt to touch his hand.

"Are you ever going to let me see that picture you drew of me yesterday?" I ask him.

He grins as he checks the rearview mirror and switches lanes. "Didn't I say I'd show you when I was finished?"

"Yeah, but I don't believe you."

He laughs. "You don't have to believe me. That doesn't mean I won't do it."

"What if you don't finish until October or something? Will you fly back just to show me?"

"I'd do that," he says easily.

"Really?"

"Yeah. Why not?"

I start to say that the six-hour flight from San Francisco to New Jersey might be a big reason not to fly back randomly in October, but my voice gets caught in my throat when we suddenly start slowing down. There are construction signs everywhere, and the cars in front of us look like they're backed up for miles. It isn't even bumper-to-bumper traffic. No one is moving an inch.

"Shit," Eli says. "Why would the GPS take us this way?"

"This isn't happening." I lean forward and cover my face with my hands. "This can't be happening."

My phone vibrates in my lap. It's Reina FaceTiming me. She's probably just trying to be a good best friend and wish me luck, but I can't even bring myself to answer.

"I can't miss my audition," I say, double-checking that

the time is correct. "I didn't come all the way to North Caro-lina just to miss my audition!"

"Calm down," Eli says, putting his hand on my arm. "You're not gonna miss it."

"Yes, I will. This is all karma for lying to my mom."

"No, it's not."

I don't say anything and stare at the license plate of the car in front of us, willing it to move.

"You're not gonna miss your audition," Eli repeats. "Look, it's starting to pick up again."

We start to move, but really slowly, like we're trying to drive through a lake of molasses. Everyone has to merge into one lane to get around the construction.

After what feels like years, traffic finally starts to move along, but we've still lost time. If I'm not late to my audition, I'll definitely be cutting it close.

Eli guns it the rest of the way. I don't complain about his speeding, or how he zips from lane to lane like he's in a racing video game. We won't have time to drop him off at the train station before my audition, or to talk about whether or not I'll go with him to his dad's. Eli agrees to drop me off and wait until my audition is over.

"It will last most of the day," I tell him.

He shrugs. "It's okay. I'll find a park for Geezer or something."

When we take our exit, I'm ready to fly out of the car.

And that's exactly what I do once Eli pulls into the Carolina Dance Center's parking lot.

"Fuck shit up!" he calls after me, which I guess is his way of saying good luck.

I keep running and wave my hand in the air, hoping he knows that means thank you. My dance bag slaps against my leg as my feet pound faster.

When I burst through the lobby doors, I'm exactly one minute late. There's a young guy standing behind a desk gathering papers. He's wearing a black T-shirt that says THE AVERY JOHNSON DANCE THEATER. If I wasn't in such a rush, I might ask if he's one of the company dancers. Instead I practically shout, "I know I'm late, but I'm here, and I really need to audition. Can I please sign in?"

His eyes widen, and he runs a hand through his short dreadlocks. "I'm sorry—" he starts to say, but then stops when Jeffrey Baptiste, the artistic director of the conservatory, approaches the table, seemingly out of nowhere, and says, "David, can you give me everyone's paperwork? I want to look it over while they're warming up."

I've never seen Jeffrey Baptiste in person, only in YouTube videos, where he's always so eloquent and poised. His bald head is even shinier in person, and he's wearing his trademark black blazer with slim-fit jeans.

I stare at him, starstruck. After a few seconds, he finally notices me.

"Can I help you?" he asks. His eyes go to the dance bag over my shoulder. "Audition sign-in ended already."

"I know, I'm really sorry." I stand up straighter and fight the urge to smooth down my hair. "There was construction on my way here, and traffic was really backed up."

"That's an excuse," he says, taking the paperwork. He doesn't look at me when he says, "Come back next year, and come back *on time*."

I feel like I've just been hit by a bus.

Jeffrey Baptiste turns around and walks down the hallway without another word. David gives me a sad smile. Neither of them knows that I won't be able to come back next year. This is it for me.

I stand there, feeling the heat gather in my cheeks, wiping away tears. Maybe if this happened on Saturday, when I'd originally planned to audition, I would have turned around and left, hopeless and defeated.

But I think of Trey's and Larissa's words. Be fierce. Believe in yourself.

And then Eli's advice: *fuck shit up*. If I left without auditioning, I'd be doing the complete opposite.

"You'll regret not letting me audition," I call down the hallway to Jeffrey.

He turns around slowly. He raises an eyebrow and looks me up and down. "Excuse me?"

"I said you'll regret it if you don't let me audition." My

voice shakes a little. I have no idea what I'm even saying. And I'm saying this to Jeffrey Baptiste, of all people! But there's no way I'm leaving without auditioning.

He doubles back so that he's standing by the table again. David's eyes dart between us like he's about to witness a snake swallow a mouse.

"Is that so?" Jeffrey says.

"Yes." I force myself to look him in the eyes. "I'm really good. And one day you'll see me dancing with another company, and you'll think back to this moment and wish you'd never turned me away."

It's like a confident and fearless version of myself has taken control of everything I do and say.

I swear, for a second it almost looks like Jeffrey smiles at me. "What's your name, young lady?"

"Chloe Pierce."

He eyes me for a few agonizing seconds. My heart hammers in my chest.

Finally, he says, "You have *one minute* to change into your shoes to warm up. No more, no less."

Did he just say what I think he said?

I don't know what made him change his mind, but I don't let him second-guess his decision.

"Thankyousomuch," I say.

I race down the hallway like my life depends on it. Which I guess it does.

"Wait!" David chases after me. He hands me a number

to pin to my chest. He smiles at me, genuinely happy this time.

"Merde," he whispers, which is what dancers say to each other instead of good luck.

Luck. I can't believe I've received so much.

Chapter 21

Merde

The studio room is huge, at least twice the size of the studios at the Philadelphia Center for Dance. There are a few boys here, but mostly girls, and more than half of the dancers are Black. Something about that helps me relax. The best part is that everyone is dressed in simple leotards and tights. No one is wearing my Homecoming dress.

I quickly claim a space at the barre and begin stretching. A hush falls over the room as Avery Johnson and Jeffrey Baptiste walk through the door. Avery Johnson is even more striking in person. He's tall, and his deep-brown skin is luminous.

"I am so, so very happy to see all of you," he says. "When I decided to start my own conservatory, I never thought so many students would want to enroll." He looks around the room and his eyes fall on each and every one of us. When he looks at me, I hold my breath. "Some have said that starting a dance school is a risk that I'm not ready to take, but at every audition I've seen so much talent, and I've been completely blown away. I'm so thankful that you're here today and that you believe in my vision." His smile widens. "I guess my point is that no matter what happens today, you should continue to follow your dreams. That's the only reason I'm standing in front of you right now."

Real-life Avery Johnson is nothing like the cruel version in my dreams. I didn't really expect him to walk around the room, examine us, and then tell me to do a bunch of *fouettés*, but it's a relief that it won't happen.

Jeffrey Baptiste quickly takes over and gives us the audition rundown. We'll start with barre exercises, then move on to center work, and we'll end with learning a piece. Our audition instructor is Alina Pavlova. She used to dance with the Joffrey Ballet, and she'll also be an instructor at the conservatory. Now there are three people we need to impress.

When we begin barre exercises, Alina walks around and surveys us, correcting some people as she passes by. As she gets closer to me, I feel my muscles tense up, but I remind myself that I just did barre exercises yesterday, and practically every day of my life. There's no reason for me to be tense. I relax my limbs and trust that my body knows what it's supposed to do. When Alina passes me as I *grand plié*, she nods. I let out a sigh of relief.

We move on to center work and spread out in rows in the middle of the floor so that Avery Johnson and Jeffrey

Baptiste, who are sitting in the front of the room, can see all of us easily. I try my best not to look at Avery too much so that I won't lose focus. The one time I glance at him, his eyes are scanning the room, and he's listening intently as Jeffrey whispers something in his ear.

We begin center work with *tendu* exercises and then switch to *adagio* combinations, which are slow movements that give us the chance to show our technique, fluidity, and strength. Alina corrects more people this time, placing her hand on one girl's back and telling her to elongate, or tapping one boy's elbows when they aren't perfectly rounded. I start to worry that I might be making the same mistakes, too, but I hear Trey's voice in my head: *Once fierce, always fierce.* I take a deep breath and go with the flow of the music. Alina never comes over to correct me.

My relief turns to dread when it's time for us to break into groups for turn combinations. No *fouettés*, thank goodness. But I try to shake away the thought that my nightmare could become reality as I do *piqués*, lame ducks, and *chaînés* across the floor. When I finish without falling out, or, more importantly, without snapping my ankle, I grin so hard it feels like my cheeks might split. Breathlessly, I scurry off to the side of the studio as the next group of dancers takes the floor.

After what feels like a thousand more combinations, we take a ten-minute break. Everyone is whispering excitedly to each other. I stand off to the side, itching to do a million things: call Reina and tell her how amazing it is to see Avery

Johnson in person, tell Larissa that she would have loved Alina Pavlova, run outside and shout to someone, anyone, that my nightmare didn't come true. A few seconds pass, and I realize that the person I most want to talk to is Eli.

The last part of our audition involves learning a piece Alina choreographed. It's more contemporary than classical. We're split into groups of three, and I get placed in the same group as a boy and a girl, both of whom I've noticed are really talented. I fight the urge to bend down and adjust my ribbons to hide my scar.

When the music starts, I trick my body into feeling as light as a feather. I pretend that I'm dancing to my own playlists, and that I'm the only one here. I forget that Avery Johnson and the rest of the dancers are watching me. I'm in my own world as I dance, as if I created the piece myself. And then as I prep and *chassé* for the *tour jeté*—I slip.

I catch myself before completely falling, but that doesn't stop a collective gasp from spreading around the room. I quickly find my footing again and continue the piece, but I feel like someone has thrown cold water all over my body. I'm no longer in my own world. I'm glaringly aware that I'm at my audition, dancing in front of Avery Johnson, and I just messed up.

You'll never be the dancer you once were.

The horrible words are back.

How could this have happened? I spent so much time worrying about the silly *fouettés* from my dreams that I never considered I would falter on something as simple as a *chassé*. I wouldn't have made a mistake like this two years ago. This is worse than any nightmare. I'm struggling to hold back tears, but then I hear another voice that's louder and clearer than my doctor's telling me I'd never dance the same again. My own.

It starts here.

I can't shout it the way I did yesterday or hold my hand over my heart. But I can recognize that those words are true.

Maybe I wouldn't have slipped if this were two years ago, or if I'd never broken my ankle. Or maybe I would have. I'll never know. I can't go back into the past and change what happened to me. Maybe it isn't such a bad thing that I'm not the dancer I was once. Otherwise, how would I grow?

I continue the piece, because all I can do right now in this moment is pull myself together and finish to the best of my ability. It starts here, with me.

When we're done, my hands are shaking as I find a place off to the side at the barre. A few dancers shoot sad glances my way, but I hold my head high. I made a mistake, but I came to this audition and gave it all I had. I'll be heartbroken if I'm not accepted, but I didn't do all of this for nothing. And if I managed to make it here, imagine how much further I can go.

My dream doesn't have to end with the conservatory. I

can still move to New York City and become a professional ballerina if I don't give up on myself.

After all the groups have danced, Avery Johnson and Jeffrey Baptiste thank everyone for coming. They tell us that we'll receive an e-mail in a couple of weeks that will let us know whether or not we've been chosen. We all file out of the studio, sweaty and exhausted. Almost every girl walks to the bathroom, and I get stuck at the end of the line. Everyone takes so long changing in the stalls that by the time I'm back in the hallway, the building is almost empty. I rush to the lobby, so busy trying to make sure Eli doesn't miss his train that when Avery Johnson rounds the corner, I crash right into him. My bag drops at his feet.

"Oh my God, I'm so sorry," I say quickly.

Avery Johnson smiles and bends down to hand me my bag. "In a bit of a hurry?"

I shake my head. "No, not really. I mean, yes, I sort of am. Not a huge rush, though." I let out a nervous laugh.

Dear Lord, I'm finally talking to *Avery Johnson*, and I can't even give him a straight answer to a yes-or-no question!

"Get home safe, all right? Thank you for coming today." He smiles at me and walks away in his elegant manner, and suddenly I know that I can't let him go without saying something more. This might be my only chance.

"Um, Mr. Johnson," I call.

He stops and turns around. "Yes?"

I suck in a breath. What do I even want to say? That I

185

want him to look past the fact that I messed up? That I lied to my mom and drove miles to be here, and I wish that were enough for him to choose me?

"Um, I just wanted to say that I admire you so much, and you're my biggest role model. I even have a poster of you in my room, and every day I look at it and feel inspired. And . . . well, that's all."

What the heck did I just say? Of all things, I told him about my *poster*. Now I sound like a creep. After this, I'm going to buy duct tape to cover my mouth, because I should never be allowed to speak again.

Avery Johnson's smile returns. "Thank you. That's very nice of you to say. If we see each other again, you'll have to bring that poster so I can sign it." He winks at me. "Have a good night, Chloe."

He walks away, and all I can do is stand there and stare at his back until he turns down a side hallway.

Avery Johnson just winked at me.

He said he would sign my poster.

And, wait a second . . . *he knew my name.*

Chapter 22

Eli Has Another Idea

When I walk outside, I spot Eli leaning against my car, smoking. Geezer pokes his head out of the back seat and sniffs the air. Eli puts out his cigarette when he sees me and waves.

"Eli!" I shout, sprinting toward him.

He pushes up off of the car, and his face lights up. "What? What happened?"

I skid to a halt right in front of him. "I ran into Avery Johnson in the hall, and I told him about how he's my role model, and he said thank you, and then he smiled at me and winked! And he knew my name! He must have been looking at my paperwork before I talked to him!" My words come out in a jumbled rush. It's a miracle Eli understands anything that I've said.

"That's dope, Chlo! Does that mean you made it?"

"I don't know! I messed up some of the choreography. I think I did well otherwise, though. Honestly, I'm just so happy that I even made it here and saw him at all!"

Eli laughs, and then he hugs me. His arms are a cocoon. I try to remember every detail from this moment: the way he smells, his warm skin, the sound of his heartbeat. These are things I never want to forget.

"I'm happy if you're happy," he says into my hair.

I pull away a little so that I can look at his face, and he stares back at me. My eyes fall to his lips, but this time I don't chastise myself to look away.

This is Eli Greene. The first person I wanted to see after my audition. The boy who once broke my heart and who I forgave. Even when I thought I hated him, my feelings never really went away.

If I can be confident onstage, why can't I be confident offstage, too? I feel like I can do anything, everything. Which explains why I slowly stand on tiptoe so that my face is closer to his. He doesn't back away. My heart is pounding as I lift my hand and place it on his cheek. He lowers his hands to my waist and . . .

His phone starts ringing.

Blinking, he pulls his phone out of his pocket and frowns.

"What is it?" I ask.

"My alarm," he says. "My train comes in thirty minutes."

And just like that I come crashing right back down to Earth. "Oh yeah. Okay."

There's so much I want to say. I should tell him that I've had more fun these last few days than I've had in years. I should say that I'm not ready for our trip to be over and that I want to go with him to his dad's house. But, instead, I stand there silently staring at the ground, arguing with myself over whether or not I should say how I feel.

"I have an idea," he suddenly says.

I look up at him. "I'm listening."

"I planned to be back at my mom's by Sunday morning. If you come with me to my dad's, we can drive back to Jersey together and be there before your mom gets home." He grins and adds, "I'd almost be doing you a favor, you know. You'll get out of driving on the highway again."

"Okay," I say quickly, at the same time as he blushes and says, "But I understand if you don't want to."

We try to talk again at the same time, and we both laugh.

"I want to go with you," I say.

He smiles, almost like he's relieved. "Cool."

I just made it through the fiercest audition. Why should I let the momentum stop now? I want to tackle something else, too. "I can drive to your dad's," I say.

"Really?" He blinks. "Are you sure? It's a two-hour drive, mostly on the highway. And it's getting dark."

I nod. "I'm sure."

I don't know how to express how happy I am that our adventure isn't over yet. Next stop: Eli's dad's.

Chapter 23

Mr. Greene

By some miracle, there's not much traffic on the way to his dad's. I still can't bring myself to drive in the fast lane, but this time around Eli doesn't complain. He's pretty relaxed, but the closer we get the more fidgety he becomes. First, he begins bouncing his knees so hard that he shakes the car. Then he sifts through my glove compartment and rearranges all my loose napkins and pens. When he repeatedly flicks his lighter on and off, I know something is wrong.

"Are you okay?" I finally ask.

"Yeah," he says. "Why?"

"You won't sit still."

He closes the glove compartment and reclines his seat. "I'm fine." He stares out the window for a while. Then, "My dad's probably pissed at me."

"Why would he be pissed?"

"Because I've been avoiding his calls all week, and he left a bunch of voicemails asking when I was gonna come down."

"*What?* You said he didn't care when you got to his house as long as you got there by Saturday for the tour."

"He didn't actually say that *verbatim*, but I know it's the truth. No matter how many times he calls."

"But what if he called your mom?" I ask, starting to panic. "What if she finds out where we are and tells my mom?"

"No, he wouldn't call her," he says. "They don't talk to each other unless it has to do with money. He'd call Larissa before he'd call my mom, and, as far as I know, he hasn't called Larissa yet." He turns to me. "We're good."

That's a relief, but I'm also upset Eli didn't tell me the truth about his dad.

"Maybe your dad is pissed, but I'm sure his feelings are hurt, too," I say.

"I mean—" he starts, then stops and shakes his head. "It's hard to be around him. I always feel like he wants something out of me, like I'm not living up to his idea of what a son should be. I wasn't gonna come down here this week, but Larissa convinced me to. She said I should tell him about art school in person. I guess I respect him enough to do that. I just don't know *how* to tell him."

"Aren't you worried he's not going to pay for you to go?"

"He has to pay. It's in the custody agreement."

"Oh." I'm not sure what else to say to him. Then I get an idea. "Let's role-play."

He laughs. "No."

"Yes," I say. I make my voice deeper. "Are you ready for college, Elijah?"

He snorts. "He doesn't talk like that."

"Let me start over." I clear my throat. "So, have you thought about what electives you want to take at UNC in the fall?"

He starts to answer, but he stops and laughs. "You're right. Role-playing like this is weird."

"Role-playing? What are you talking about? It's me, your dad, trying to have a conversation with you about college."

He shakes his head, still smiling. "Okay, *Dad*, remember a couple years ago when you met my art teacher, Mr. Curtis, at that open house?" I nod. "Well, he said he thinks I have a lot of potential, and he suggested I apply to a couple art schools. So . . . I did. And I got in."

"What are you trying to tell me? That you're going to art school instead of UNC?"

"Yeah," he says. "The San Francisco Art Institute."

"I won't lie, I am surprised. But I'm proud of you for making your own decision instead of following along with what I think is best. You'll do great there." I pat him on the shoulder.

"That's definitely *not* how it will go."

"I know," I say. But I'm pushing for optimism, because we just came off the exit, and now we're driving through the beach town where Mr. Greene lives, and Eli is visibly more anxious.

I roll up my window because it's a little chilly, but not before I get a whiff of the salty air. It's darker now, so I can't see the ocean, but I can hear it. Eli directs me down street after street until we finally pull up in front of Mr. Greene's house. He has a wraparound porch. If he wants to swim in the ocean, he only has to walk a few feet from his back door.

"This is beautiful," I say.

Eli stares intently at the house and doesn't respond.

Before he opens his door, I say, "Maybe you should just show him your art. Then he'll see how important it is to you."

"Maybe," he mumbles.

He gets out, gathers his things, and puts Geezer on his leash. I follow suit, and as we're walking up the driveway, it occurs to me that I was so excited to spend more time with Eli, I never asked if it was actually okay for me to be here.

"Um, Eli," I say, "did you tell your dad I was coming?"

From the look on his face, I can tell the answer is no. I freeze, unsure if I should turn around and get back in my car. Then the porch light cuts on and the front door opens. I see Mr. Greene's silhouette in the doorway. He steps outside and peers at us. He's tall and looks so much like Eli. The only difference is that his hair is gray and his brown skin is a few shades darker. He's dressed in a crisp cardigan and slacks.

"So, you finally decided to show," he says to Eli.

Eli stops at the bottom of the porch steps. For a brief moment, he has the same look of fear and embarrassment on his face that he did when Mom caught him climbing our cherry tree years ago. Then he stands up straighter and the look disappears.

"Better late than never," he says.

Mr. Greene nods at me and raises an eyebrow. "And you brought a guest."

I blink, surprised that he doesn't recognize me.

"It's Chloe Pierce," Eli says. "Ms. Carol's daughter." When Mr. Greene doesn't say anything, Eli adds, "They live across the street from us."

Mr. Greene steps closer. I wave and say, "Hi, it's nice to see you."

"Hello," he says. His tone isn't exactly welcoming. He turns his attention back to Eli. "Elijah, what makes you think I'm actually going to let you in my house? You obviously don't respect me enough to be here when I asked you to be."

"Dad, come on."

"Don't *Dad, come on* me. Who do you think you are? I don't care if you're eighteen. You're still the child and I'm the parent. When I tell you to be somewhere, you be there. And I bet your mom has no idea where you are, does she? She probably wasn't even paying attention."

Eli narrows his eyes. "Don't bring her into it."

I take a step backward and bump into Geezer. I shouldn't be here to witness this argument. I shouldn't be here at all. What I should do is quietly walk back to my car and drive home.

"I'm here now," Eli says. "I didn't miss the tour. I don't see what the big deal is."

"You don't see what the big deal is." Mr. Greene laughs. "You've got a lot of nerve. You know that?"

"I must get it from you," Eli mumbles.

Mr. Greene's eyes flash. He looks like he wants to throttle his son. Eli stands stock-still, staring at his dad, waiting to see what he'll do. I don't know what's gotten into him. I would never talk to Mom like that in a million years.

Mr. Greene closes his eyes and takes a deep breath. When he speaks again, his voice is calmer.

"I have to continue working. We'll finish this discussion in the morning." He glances at me. "Please make up the guest room for Chloe."

Without another word, he turns around and walks inside.

All is quiet for a few seconds. I'm still reeling from witnessing their argument. Eli just stares at the doorway.

Softly, I ask, "Are you okay?"

He doesn't turn to look at me. "I'm fine."

"I thought things were going to get worse."

"Nah, that wouldn't happen," he says. "He's too obsessed with appearances. He doesn't want to be known as the Black guy on his block who screams at his son."

"Oh." I look at the houses around us. Everything about this street looks quiet and peaceful, like nothing out of the ordinary ever happens.

I follow Eli inside. The house is spacious, but it doesn't feel very lived in. I get the sense that Mr. Greene is hardly home, and whenever he's here, he spends most of his time in his office.

Wordlessly, Eli leads me upstairs to the guest room. The furniture is simple: one white dresser and one twin bed with a light blue comforter and pillows to match. All I want to do is lie down and fall asleep, but I stand in the doorway, hesitant.

"Maybe I should go," I say. "You and your dad have a lot going on. I'll just be in the way."

Eli turns around to look at me, and his eyes are red. I want to reach out and hug him.

"Stay," he says. He gently places his hand on my shoulder, like it might keep me in this spot. "Please."

How can I say no? I hadn't realized that things between him and his dad were so bad.

"Let's go for a walk," I say.

He takes a second to contemplate, but then he walks out of the room and I follow him outside.

Chapter 24

Life's a Beach

We walk around his dad's neighborhood in silence for a while. Geezer leads the way, and we turn down each street according to his whims. An ice cream truck cruises by and we flag him down for snacks. Afterward, we find ourselves looping around to his dad's street. Instead of walking up the driveway to the front door, we make our way to the backyard and head for the beach. It's completely empty except for us.

Eli lets Geezer off of his leash, and he runs down to the water but quickly makes his way back to us when he sees how far the tide comes in. Eli shrugs off his hoodie and lays it on the sand so that we can sit. I bring my knees up to my chest and run my fingers through the sand. I don't want to say anything until he's ready to talk.

He finally breaks the silence. "The only reason I decided to play basketball was because he wanted me to."

I look over at him, and he's staring straight ahead at the ocean.

"After he moved so far away, I figured he wouldn't care if I quit the team," he says. "But once he found out, he bitched about it for weeks because he thought it would make my college apps weak. I felt like everyone always wanted something from me. After I quit, it was like all of my responsibilities disappeared. I didn't have a coach to impress or teammates who depended on me. I knew my dad was disappointed, but at least the bar wasn't set so high anymore."

"Is that when you started to hang out with Isiah?" I ask.

He nods. "But after a while I realized he just wanted stuff from me, too. Rides to parties, money for alcohol. We didn't have a real friendship. I cut him off a couple months ago."

I nod, realizing this is most likely when he reconnected with Trey.

"Do you remember how hype I used to get when he'd take me fishing?" he asks. "Every trip would end with him saying how he wanted me to follow in his footsteps so that we could open our own corporate law firm. You know, *forget the man, do our own thing,* and all that."

"I used to get jealous when he took you fishing," I say, picturing the drawing he showed me in his sketchbook. Eli looks surprised, so I clarify. "I don't mean the act of going fishing. I mean because you had a dad who could do stuff like that with you. Or rather, I was jealous that you had a dad and I didn't."

He shifts so that he's facing me. "I never knew you felt that way. You never talk about him."

"I don't have much to say. I barely had a chance to know him, but after he died, I started having nightmares. My mom thinks it's because I knew something had changed and it scared me. I don't know if that's the real reason, but I still have them. I've had them all week, actually."

He cocks his head to the side, and I can tell he's thinking about when he woke me up on Tuesday morning and it was clear I'd just had a nightmare.

"Why didn't you ever tell me?" he asks.

"Honestly, I thought you'd make fun of me."

He frowns. "I wouldn't have."

"Yeah, I know that now."

"I used to think you had it easier because it was just you and your mom," he says. "You never had to worry about hearing your parents argue all the time. Does that sound weird?"

"No," I say. "It doesn't."

"I've done so many things in my life just because my parents wanted me to," he says. "But art belongs to me, it's my thing. I just want them to understand that."

"Of course they will," I say. "They love you. But first you have to tell them."

He sighs. "I don't know if I can."

"Don't doubt yourself."

He gives me a small smile, and once again my eyes fall to his lips. When I get goose bumps, I convince myself it's because of the chilly breeze.

"We should head back," he says, standing up. I stand,

too, and he shakes the sand out of his hoodie and hands it to me. He calls Geezer, and then we make our way back inside.

Eli walks me upstairs and we pause in front of the guest room. I give him his hoodie back.

"Thank you for staying," he says.

"Of course."

We stare at each other. The last time he thanked me for something, we were standing face-to-face just like this. That day, I was waiting for a drawing. Now I'm waiting for something else. I almost kissed him earlier today, and he almost let me. The ball is in his court.

He leans forward, and I hold my breath. He's about to kiss me. It's really happening. I close my eyes and angle my face toward his.

He does kiss me. But not on the lips. *On my cheek.*

This will forever be marked as the day that I nearly died of embarrassment and disappointment.

Maybe we're just meant to be friends. That's better than being enemies.

I just need to learn to be okay with it.

"Good night, Chlo," he says.

I force a smile. "Good night, Eli."

I'm dreaming. It's a good dream. Eli and I are *finally* kissing. He pulls away and whispers my name. I don't know how long it takes me to realize that he's whispering my name in real life. I open my eyes, and he's standing in the doorway.

"What are you doing here?" I ask, sitting up. The time on my phone says it's 12:32 a.m.

He walks over and crouches beside the bed. He looks anxious. "I have to tell you something."

"Tell me what?" I glance at the hallway, nervous that his dad will wake up and catch us in the same room. "What's wrong?"

He takes a deep breath. Then: "Do you always sleep with that on your head? You look like a baker."

I readjust my bonnet. "Is that what you came in here to tell me?"

"No, no." He shakes his head. "What I want to say is that there's a reason I asked to be your date to Homecoming."

I go completely still. "What?"

"There's a reason I asked to go to Homecoming with you," he repeats. "And there is a reason I gave you that drawing that day at your locker, and there's a reason I could have easily taken a bus or a train to my dad's, but I asked if you would give me a ride instead."

My heart pounds as I absorb his words.

"I like you," he says. "I've probably liked you ever since you stuck your hand in that bush for my house keys. You didn't even cry when you cut your arm." He pauses. "I know I was an asshole for tricking you into doing it."

"You like me," I repeat, not quite believing what's happening.

"Yeah, and when you told me you were going to the dance, I kept picturing you dancing with someone else, and I didn't want that to happen, so I asked if I could go with you, even though I hate school dances, because they never play any good music, but you were going, and you said I could be your date, and I was happy, but then I fucked it up. I should have told you earlier tonight, or yesterday, or—"

"Eli, stop," I say. "I like you, too."

He pauses, blinking. "You do?"

"Why do you sound so surprised? I almost kissed you earlier! I thought it was obvious!"

"It wasn't obvious!" He frowns. "Or maybe it was. I don't know. I was mainly focusing on the fact that you were letting me hug you."

I shake my head, smiling. "You're so oblivious."

"I know," he says softly.

He moves closer, bringing one hand up to cup my cheek. Time slows. I don't move as he leans down so that his lips are level with mine. We stare at each other, transfixed.

"Chlo," he says, "can I kiss you?"

I nod slowly. Then his lips are on mine. They're soft and taste surprisingly like vanilla. We stay still with our lips gently pressed against each other. Then he brings me closer and kisses me deeper.

This is what it feels like to kiss Eli Greene: floating higher and higher until I land on another planet.

We pull away and smile at each other. It's almost like if one of us speaks the wonder of this moment will disappear.

"I noticed something," he finally says. "You haven't twitched your nose in, like, three days."

"That's because you haven't done anything to annoy me."

He laughs. "Can I sit next to you?"

I make room for him, and we sit shoulder to shoulder. He reaches out and takes my hand in both of his. Now I finally know what it's like to hold his hand for real.

I lay my head on his shoulder. Just as I'm beginning to fall asleep again, he says, "You have to come visit me in San Francisco."

I feel myself smile. "And you have to come visit me in New York City."

"Okay. But Geezer has to come, too."

"Of course he does. Deal?"

"Deal."

Chapter 25

Eavesdrop

THURSDAY

When I wake up in the morning, Eli is gone. It's the first night this week that I haven't had any nightmares. I lie in bed for a few minutes, remembering how natural it felt to kiss him, to hold his hand.

I get up and open the bedroom door, planning to head to the bathroom, but I stop short when I overhear Eli and his dad arguing downstairs in the living room.

"Art school?" Mr. Greene says, his voice booming. "Are you out of your damn mind?"

"No," Eli replies calmly. "I'm not."

I back up and flatten myself against the wall. I don't know why I do that, since neither of them can see me at the top of the stairs. But I know this is a private conversation that isn't meant to be overheard. I should shut myself in the guest room until they're finished, but I don't move. Even though Eli doesn't know I'm standing here, I want to support him. Geezer trots through the living room and plops down at the foot of the stairs. I take a further step back so even he won't notice me.

"What do you think you're going to do with an art degree?" Mr. Greene asks. "You think you're going to sell paintings and earn enough to survive? I'll be the first to tell you that crap isn't realistic. That's the problem with your generation. You want everything in the world, but none of you want to *work* for it. If you think I'm going to take care of you and pay your bills for the rest of your life, you're wrong."

"I'm not a painter," Eli says. "I won't be selling any paintings."

I jump when I hear my phone vibrating on the bedside table in the guest room. I close the door so they won't hear it, too.

"Then what is it, exactly, that you plan on doing?" Mr. Greene asks.

"I don't know, Dad. That's why I'm going to art school, so I can figure it out." Eli pauses. "I was thinking I might get a couple of my sketches printed on some T-shirts and sell them. Maybe on hoodies, too."

Mr. Greene scoffs. "T-shirts and hoodies. You've got to be kidding me."

"No, I'm not kidding," Eli says, his voice slightly rising. I'm worried that he'll get angrier and their conversation will escalate into a shouting match. But, instead, Eli says, "Here . . . just look at this. Please."

He must be handing over his sketchbook. It gets quiet,

and I hear the sound of pages turning. I wish I could see Mr. Greene's expression right now.

"It's obvious how much work you put into your art, Elijah," Mr. Greene says, "but being an artist doesn't guarantee stability or security. This is something you can do on the side. It shouldn't be your main focus. You came down here so we could visit UNC, and that's what we're doing."

"This is my life, and this is what I want to do," Eli says earnestly. "Can't you respect that I'm trying to take responsibility for my future? You're always pushing me to grow up and be a man. Now you have to let me try and be one."

Mr. Greene sighs loudly. "Elijah, you—"

A crashing sound interrupts him. I dash back into the guest room to find that my phone vibrated its way onto the floor. Reina is calling me. I completely forgot to call her after my audition. I close the door and call her back.

"Don't be mad at me," I say when she picks up.

"Chlo, oh my God, where are you?"

"I'm at Eli's dad's house. Why?"

"What?!" she shrieks. "Why aren't you on your way home? Your mom is going to *kill* you!"

"No, she's not," I say slowly. I have no idea why she's freaking out. "She doesn't fly in until Sunday evening. I'll be home by then."

Reina pauses. "Oh no. Don't tell me you haven't talked to her yet."

The way she says it makes my stomach drop. "No. What's going on?"

She inhales deeply. "Okay, so your mom called me, and I started to act like I was my mom, but she told me she knew I wasn't my mom because she went to *my house* looking for you, and my parents told her neither of us had been there all week!"

"She's *home*?"

I feel like I can't breathe.

"Yes! I don't know what happened! She came back early for some reason. I called you as soon as I found out, but you weren't answering. Your mom is so freaking scary I couldn't even come up with a good lie!"

"Oh my God." I scroll past my missed alerts from Reina and see missed calls, texts, and voicemails from Mom. "Oh my God."

"My mom is gonna kick my *ass* once I get home," Reina cries. "She said I impersonated her and that I should go to jail! I'm her daughter, for Christ's sake!"

The room is spinning. Mom is home. She knows I'm not with Reina. "I have to call you back."

I hang up and read all of Mom's texts.

Hi, baby. We're on our way home from the airport. Jean-Marc got food poisoning, so we flew back once the cruise stopped in the Bahamas. You're probably still sleeping. Give me a call when you wake up.

> Just left you a voicemail. We're in an Uber on our way
> home. Meet me there?

The next few messages all came within the span of fifteen minutes.

> Are you and Reina at her house? I'll stop by and
> take you to breakfast.
>
> Just got home. Call me when you get this.
>
> Chloe, baby, pick up. I'm worried. I'm going to
> drive over there.
>
> You lied to me?! Mrs. Acosta says you haven't been
> there all week! Where are you? Call me back ASAP!
>
> Chloe, this isn't a game. Call me back right now!

She calls again as I'm reading her last text. I freeze. I know I have to answer because I don't want her to think something terrible happened to me. But I'm afraid. My hands are shaking so badly I almost drop my phone. I take a deep breath and try to get it together. But no deep-breathing techniques will prepare me for this conversation. I answer the phone before I chicken out.

"Mom, I'm safe. I'm okay. I'm—"

"Where are you?!"

"I'm in—"

"You've got me ready to call the cops! How could you lie to me like this? Reina has been at camp! Where are *you*?"

I gulp. "I'm in North Carolina."

"WHAT?" she yells so loudly I have to pull the phone away from my ear. "What the hell are you doing in *North Carolina*?!"

A few days ago, Eli said he thought Mom hated him, and I told him that wasn't true. I hope she doesn't start to hate him today.

"I'm with Eli," I say. "We're at his dad's house."

"Eli?" Bewilderment cuts through her anger. "Linda's son?"

"Yes."

She's silent. Then: "I'm coming down there to get you."

No, no, no. "Mom, you don't have to come get me. I'll leave right now."

"No, I'm coming to get you like I said."

"If you come pick me up, then how will we get my car back to New Jersey?" I ask. She pauses, and I take my chance to swoop in on her hesitation. "I can drive back. I'm leaving right now. I swear."

"You'd better leave right now and have your behind back here *today*. Or else I *will* come down there and bring you back here myself, and I won't care about leaving your car there since you can't be trusted with it anyway. Do you understand me?"

"Yes, ma'am." I frantically start shoving everything in my duffel bag.

"I am so disappointed in you, Chloe." She doesn't sound angry anymore, just sad and tired. She adds, "Please drive safely."

Then she hangs up.

I can take her being mad at me. I expected that. But I didn't expect her to be disappointed. That brings on an entire new wave of guilt that settles deep in the pit of my stomach. She wasn't supposed to find out this way. I was supposed to have time to figure out how to tell her the truth.

I shove on my Chucks and throw my bag over my shoulder. When I walk downstairs, Eli and his dad are still in a heated argument. They pause and look at me in surprise.

"What's wrong?" Eli asks, crossing the room in quick strides. Quietly, he asks, "Why are you crying?"

I wipe my cheeks, startled. I hadn't even realized I was crying. Mr. Greene stares at us, concerned. Eli takes my hand and leads me into the kitchen.

"Tell me what's wrong," he says.

"My mom knows where I am." A sob threatens to escape, but I take a deep breath and hold it in. "I have to go home."

His eyes get huge. "Shit. Shit. Fucking shit." He runs a hand over his face and groans. "Of course this week would end with me getting you in fucking trouble."

"Wait, what are you talking about? None of this is your fault."

"Yes, it is. *I* asked you to take me with you to D.C. *I* crashed your car. *I'm* the reason you had to come to North Carolina to audition. And now your mom's gonna hate me more than she already does."

"Stop saying that! She doesn't hate you."

He gives me a look that says *bullshit*.

"She *doesn't*." I don't know who I'm trying to convince more, me or him.

"I'm coming with you," he says. "I'll get Geezer. I'll tell my dad we have to leave because of an emergency or something." He starts to turn away.

"No, you need to stay." I grab his arm and pull him back toward me. "You can't leave things like this with your dad."

He shakes his head, but he doesn't verbally deny what I've said. "I'm not going to let you drive all the way back to Jersey by yourself. You're scared of the damn highway!"

"Well, it's about time I got over that fear. I drove here, didn't I?"

"I'm leaving with you," he insists. "I can come back and see my dad another time. Just give me a few minutes to pack my stuff. Fuck, I need to make sure Geezer uses the bathroom."

"No." I jump in his way. "You're staying. I'm leaving. End of story."

"Don't tell me what to do." He narrows his eyes. Of course we choose right now of all moments to argue.

Then I realize we might not have many more moments for stupid arguments. Mom will probably ground me until Eli leaves for college.

I quickly reach out and hug him close. At first, he's surprised, but then he wraps his arms around me. I take in his fresh-laundry scent, the slight hint of cigarette smoke. I'll think about this during the eight-hour drive back to Jersey.

Oh my God. *Eight hours.*

"Please stay with your dad," I say, pulling away. "He needs to understand why art school is so important to you, and I don't want to be the reason that you decide to leave. I'll be fine, I swear."

He sighs. It's heavy and full of reluctance. "I don't like this."

"Me neither." I make myself smile in hopes that he'll worry about me less. "But don't be so dramatic. I'll see you in a few days."

He smirks, but his eyes look sad. "I might see you if they don't lock you up for driving so slow on the highway."

"Shut up."

I punch his shoulder lightly. He catches my fist in his hands and cradles it in his palms. "Be careful."

"I will."

Mr. Greene is confused by my abrupt departure, but he gives me water bottles and snacks for the road. He makes me promise to call and check in every few hours.

Eli walks me to my car, and Geezer trails happily behind us, no doubt thinking it's time for another adventure. I bend down and scratch behind his ears as Eli places my bag in the passenger seat. Geezer closes his eyes and lets his tongue hang out of his mouth.

I give him one last good scratch. "Who would have thought we'd become friends, huh?"

Geezer whines when I get in the car and don't open the back-seat door for him.

"Damn, Geezer. Don't start liking her better than me," Eli says, coming to stand at my window. He looks at me. "If your mom locks you up in your room, I'll come save you."

"How will you do that?"

His wolfish grin makes a reappearance. "It'll be a surprise."

I smile and shake my head. "I don't know how I feel about that."

"You'll like it. I promise."

He bends down, and with his index finger, he tilts my chin up and kisses me. For a brief second, I forget how much trouble I'm in, and that Mom is waiting for me at home. I forget that I'll have to drive on the highway for a third of a day.

When he pulls away, it feels too soon.

"Remember, this all happened for a reason," he says. "I'll see you Sunday for Easter dinner."

I appreciate how he says it with such conviction, like there isn't a chance that the only way I'll see him Sunday is if I'm looking at him through my window.

I know I'm basically dead meat, but I don't regret anything about the past few days. Too many good things have happened for me not to feel the least bit hopeful.

So I repeat, "See you Sunday."

Chapter 26

Lost and Found

My mom is cautious because, according to her, my dad was not.

Well, that's not the right place to start their story.

My mom was always cautious, even before they met. That's why she became a nurse. Cautious people work well in hospitals.

She met my dad during a completely normal overnight shift. He'd almost cut off the tip of his finger while chopping onions. She asked if he'd been drinking at the time, and he told her no. He simply got distracted by the television and wasn't paying attention. He told her he was a car salesman. It explained why he was an easy talker. He had a nice smile. She liked him almost immediately.

While my mom assessed his wound, they talked about where they were from, their favorite music and movies, places they'd like to see. My dad hadn't traveled much yet, but he wanted to see the world. Jokingly, he'd asked if my mom would join him. She said no, she barely even knew him. But she was surprised by how much she wanted to say yes.

Later, in the early morning hours, after my dad received his stitches and my mom's shift ended, my dad waited for her in the lobby. He asked if she'd like to come over and he'd cook her breakfast as a way to thank her. She agreed, but only if she could do the chopping. She soon learned that my dad was prone to accidents. He was constantly bumping into walls, or tripping and falling. He was excitable and easily distracted. Mom was always there to bandage him up. Eventually, I was born, and my dad tried to be more cautious for my sake. Mom says he was careful never to drop me.

The night my dad died, he'd stayed late at work and he was eager to get home. He stopped at an intersection, and when he had the green light, he hit the gas. He didn't see the truck coming. It had run a red light, right into the driver's side. The police later told my mom that my dad was killed on impact.

All she had left was me, a three-year-old who hadn't even had the chance to really know her father, and who couldn't sleep at night anymore. Between working and raising me alone, her hands were full. Ms. Linda urged her to sign me up for ballet to give herself a break.

The first time I performed in front of a crowd I was a five-year-old Tiny Tot. We wore flower costumes and danced to "It Might as Well Be Spring" at the annual spring fair on South Street. I remember spotting Mom in the crowd and seeing the proud smile on her face. I felt like I'd accomplished something for those few minutes. She didn't smile very often.

After the performance, she wanted to take me home, but I begged her to walk with me around the fair. She agreed to stay, but only for a little bit. We strolled hand in hand until Mom paused in front of a jewelry stand. While she browsed, I noticed a clown making balloon animals a few feet away. A group of children surrounded him. I wandered closer, fascinated as he looped and tied a butterfly's wings.

When I turned back, Mom wasn't behind me anymore. I looked up at the faces above me and didn't recognize anyone.

There is nothing worse than realizing that you're lost. I burst into tears. A woman paused in front of me and asked what was wrong. I tried to tell her that I was looking for my mom, but I couldn't stop crying.

Then I heard Mom calling me. She pushed her way through the crowd and gathered me into her arms. Her hands were shaking as she rubbed my back. She'd been just as afraid as me. That was the first time that I'd ever felt guilty.

"Don't you ever do that to me again," she whispered, holding me tighter. "Don't ever do that again."

Chapter 27

Now or Never

The drive home is exhausting, but I'm less afraid of the road than I thought I'd be. Maybe it's because the road will be nothing compared to my confrontation with Mom. I put on a special Beyoncé playlist to help me feel strong, but it only makes me think that when Beyoncé was my age, she was busy touring the world, doing exactly what she loved.

I pull over at a rest stop in Maryland to get gas and call Mom to let her know where I am. She's still just as angry as she was this morning. Curtly, she tells me to drive safely and then hangs up. I was about to open a bag of chips, but her tone makes me lose my appetite.

I text Eli, In Maryland. How are things with your dad?

He texts back, *glad you're safe. we're still touring UNC tomorrow, so not making a lot of progress. he did say he liked my art tho*

That's a start.

Geezer misses you and I guess I do too

I miss you too, I guess. I miss Geezer more.

That's messed up

I'm just being honest.

We text back and forth for a little before I take a quick power nap and get back on the road.

It's a little after nine p.m. when I finally reach New Jersey. My hearts pounds as I enter my neighborhood and turn onto my street. I slow to a creep as I pull into the driveway. The light is on in the living room.

As I walk toward the door, I try to rehearse what I'll say to Mom.

Mom, I know you're upset, but I went to North Carolina for a good reason. I auditioned for Avery Johnson's conservatory, and he talked to me! You should be proud of me!

Mom, I know I lied to you. But this is the first time I've lied to you my whole life. Can you let this one go?

Mom, just tell me how long you're going to ground me for.

I have no idea what I'll say. I'm not the five-year-old who got lost at a fair. I'm seventeen, and I did this on my own. There will be no easy forgiveness.

I take a deep breath and walk through the door. The hallway is empty. For some reason, I expected Mom to be waiting for me there. I keep walking and turn into the living room. Jean-Marc is snoring on the couch with a jug of water and a box of saltine crackers on the coffee table in front of him. I drop my bag at my feet, and he stirs awake. He blinks at me a few times, then his eyes get wide. He whispers, "You are in trouble, missy."

"Chloe, come in here!" Mom yells from the kitchen.

I whip around toward the sound of her voice and slowly make my way to her.

Mom is sitting at the table, holding an empty tea mug. Her posture is rigid, and her mouth is set in a thin line. But she got a tan. Vacation must have been good to her in some way. She doesn't give me a chance to ask if this is true.

"Do you know how worried I was about you?" she says, her voice rising immediately. "Do you know how terrified I was when I found out you weren't at Reina's house? I'm trying to wrap my mind around why you'd drive all the way to North Carolina with Eli." She shakes her head. "What you did was so stupid."

"Mom—"

"And Linda had no idea you were with Eli, by the way. I guess he must have lied to her, too. Was that all a part of your spring break plan?" she asks. "Lie to your parents so you can go on a little road trip?" She pauses and squints at me. "Is something going on between you two that I never knew about?"

"No!" Heat creeps up my neck and spreads across my cheeks. "That's not why we went."

"Then *tell me* why."

It's now or never. I take a deep breath and start from the beginning with my original plan to audition in D.C. By the time I'm finished, Mom's arms, which were crossed, have fallen to her sides. She stares at me, eyes wide. Then she scrunches up her face, like she's trying to understand what I've said.

"You auditioned?" she asks, blinking.

"Yes, Mom. I had to." I cringe at the desperation in my voice. "I swear I was going to tell you everything if I got into the conservatory. I hate that you had to find out like this."

Her confused expression morphs into fury. "You knew how I felt about you auditioning. I can't believe you went behind my back and did it anyway. And on top of that you got into an accident! Why would you even think to let Eli drive your car? Lord knows that boy is always up to no good, Chloe."

I start to defend him, but I know now isn't the time.

Her teakettle whistles, and we both jump. She walks to the stove and pours the hot water into her mug. With her back to me, she says, "You're not going to that conservatory if you're accepted."

Her words are a punch to the gut.

"Mom, you know how important this is to me," I say. "I didn't train so many years just to throw it all away."

"Nobody says you have to throw it away."

"I won't be happy staying in New Jersey or going to college and taking dance classes on the side. You know that isn't what I want. New York is the best place to be for my career."

She glances back at me and shakes her head. "I'm not going to keep going back and forth with you. I said no."

This isn't even about whether or not she'll let me go to the conservatory anymore.

It's about her blatantly refusing to support my dream.

She can't do this to me. She *can't*.

"You can't keep me here!" I hear myself shout.

She spins around and looks at me like I've lost my mind. I guess I must have, because I keep going.

"You have this ridiculous idea that something bad will happen to me because of what happened to my dad, but that doesn't make any sense and it's not fair! I'll be eighteen by the time I graduate, and, with or without the conservatory *or* your permission, I'll move to New York City and you won't be able to stop me."

She blinks and opens her mouth, but no words come out. A distant part of me feels bad about bringing up my dad this way, but I can't make myself apologize, and I can't hold back any of my anger.

"And why didn't you tell me that Eli came to see me after my surgery?" I ask. "He wanted to apologize, and you turned him away. I never even knew."

She stares at me for a second, holding her steaming tea mug in silence. When she finally speaks, her voice is level. "All I know is that Eli was supposed to take you to a dance, and the next time I saw you, you had a broken ankle and he was nowhere to be found. And, please, he only lives across the street. What stopped him from coming back more than once to see you?" She pauses like she wants me to answer. When

I don't, she continues. "And yes, Chloe, by the time you graduate, you will be an adult with the right to do whatever you please, but right now you are still my responsibility, and I say that you're not going to this conservatory, and that's final."

My anger recedes to make room for my heartbreak. "Mom, please—"

"And give me your car keys," she says, cutting me off. "You're grounded."

Wordlessly, I hand them over. I'm fuming, miserable, and exhausted all at once. After everything, I can't believe that this is happening.

She puts my keys in her pocket.

"I'm going to sleep," she says. "You should, too. You've had a long drive."

I step aside as she passes me. She walks upstairs and minutes later I hear her bedroom door open and close.

I stand in the kitchen, shaking. I swipe at the tears falling down my cheeks and walk into the living room to get my duffel bag. Jean-Marc is wide awake now, munching on his crackers. He takes one look at me and slides over to make room on the couch. When I sit down, he holds out his sleeve of crackers, and I take some. I realize I haven't eaten anything in hours, and I'm starving.

After a few silent minutes of me wiping away my tears, Jean-Marc says, "Did you have fun at least?"

I check over my shoulder to make sure Mom isn't around. "Yes."

His booming laugh fills the entire room.

"I'm sorry you got sick," I say.

"Well, now I know not to eat shellfish on vacation." He smiles softly. "Don't worry about your mom. She'll come around."

His sympathy only makes me cry harder.

"Aww, come on now. No tears." He hugs me with one arm and offers another cracker. "She loves you. She's angry because she was afraid. Just give her some time."

I wish I could believe him.

Through tears, I say, "I hope you're right."

Chapter 28

Quarantined

FRIDAY

Last night I dreamt of nothing because I didn't sleep. I kept thinking about how hopeful I felt after I auditioned. My world was large and full of possibility. Now it's tiny again, so small you'd need a microscope to see it. Why did I ever think I could convince Mom to let me go to the conservatory? I was so delusional. I've been crying so much my face is swollen.

The only good thing is Mom didn't take my phone. I guess she doesn't have enough experience grounding me to know that's what most parents do. I called Eli last night to tell him what happened, but he didn't answer. A little while later, I texted him and he never responded.

I call Reina first thing in the morning to check in on her. I hope she's not in as much trouble as me.

"Reina can't talk right now," Mr. Acosta says, answering Reina's phone. "She's grounded. Call back in two weeks."

Well, that makes two of us.

I quarantine myself to my room all morning and afternoon. I can hear Mom moving around, making meals, watching television, but I stay put. I only leave to go to the bathroom. Thank goodness for the snacks Mr. Greene gave me yesterday. Otherwise, I'd starve.

Then it's almost three p.m. Time for ballet. Usually, I drive myself to the dance studio right after school, but I'm grounded and can't drive my own car. I brace myself as I walk down the hall to Mom's room. She's sitting on her bed with her laptop perched on her lap. She's clicking through vacation photos. I see her lying on the beach and standing on the deck of the cruise ship. In each picture she looks so happy and relaxed. I can't remember the last time I saw her look like that. How awful it must have been to leave paradise and come home to find your daughter gone.

How awful it is to be the one who's grounded.

"Mom, I need a ride to ballet," I say.

She startles and turns to face me. She quickly closes her laptop. "I can take you, but I picked up a late shift at the hospital. Jean-Marc can bring you home."

I stand there awkwardly, silently fuming. "Okay, thanks."

The drive to Philly is tense. I can't remember the last time I was angry like this at Mom. I can't remember the last time she was angry with me. Stevie Wonder plays on the radio, and Mom doesn't even hum along, even though she loves his music.

I want to apologize for bringing up my dad in our

argument last night, but I can't. I meant what I said, and apologizing would be like admitting defeat.

When Mom finally pulls into the dance studio parking lot, I can't get out of the car soon enough.

"Jean-Marc will pick you up and take you straight home," she says. "You aren't allowed to go anywhere else. Understood?"

"Yes."

"Good." She looks like she wants to say something else, but she rolls up her window and drives away.

I stare at the studio building and fight to remind myself why I'm here: I love ballet. It means everything to me.

But having Mom's support means everything to me, too, and I don't have it.

❧

I try to get out of my own head during class, but it's hard. With each turn and combination, I catch glimpses of my disappointment in the mirror. After class ends, I take an unnecessarily long time to untie my pointe shoes. Jean-Marc is in the parking lot, waiting to take me home, and once I get there, I won't be able to see the outside world again. I'm milking this time for all it's worth.

I'm slowly putting my pointe shoes in my bag when Miss Dana walks over to me.

"Where've you been all week?" she asks. "I thought you might be sick."

I look up at her. "I wasn't sick," I say.

She waits for further explanation.

I contemplate if it's worth telling her where I've really been, what I've done. The story doesn't have a happy ending. But Miss Dana is the one who encouraged me to audition in the first place. I owe it to her. So, I tell her everything. Well, the parts that matter. I leave out all the details about Eli and me.

"I knew something was different about you," Miss Dana says once I finish. "When you walked into the room today, you held your head up high and you looked *ready*. I haven't seen you look like that in a long time."

"Really?" I sit up straighter.

"Yeah, you used to have this confidence about you, but after you got hurt, you lost it a little," she says. "But today it's back, and it's stronger than before. I'm not happy that you lied to your mom, but I'm proud of you for auditioning. You should be proud of yourself. too."

"I am," I say, truly meaning it.

On the ride home, Jean-Marc is his usual chipper self. He tries to make small talk and offers to take me for ice cream. Usually, I'd jump at the chance, but I don't have the appetite.

My phone vibrates, and I rush to pull it out of my bag, hoping that it's Eli. But it's just Mom, texting to make sure that Jean-Marc picked me up. Disappointed is an understatement.

I don't know what's up with Eli or why he hasn't

responded to my texts. I can't imagine he's that busy with his dad. Maybe he's planning to save me from being locked away in my room, like he said. A girl can dream.

As we turn onto our street, Ms. Linda is getting out of her car. She sees us approaching, and she pauses as she walks up her driveway. She is the last person I want to see right now. I'm sure she's angry with me, too.

It takes everything in me not to duck down.

"Can you go around the block?" I ask Jean-Marc.

He glances at me. "What? Why?"

"Please!" I shout. Then I lower my voice. "Please, please drive around the block. I can't talk to her right now."

I look over at Ms. Linda and Jean-Marc follows my line of sight. Wordlessly, he continues to drive past my house, giving Ms. Linda a little wave.

"Thank you," I say, once we turn the corner.

"You know you'll have to talk to her eventually."

"I know." I sigh.

Eventually it will be Sunday evening. The thought of having Easter dinner with both Mom and Ms. Linda is unbearable.

Later that night, I'm lying in bed when my phone chimes. I dive for it, but it's not a text from Eli. It's from Larissa.

Eli told me your mom found out about the trip. Are you okay?

Well, the good news is that if Larissa talked to him, there's proof he's alive and didn't lose his phone at the UNC campus or in some weird fishing accident. The bad news is he's clearly avoiding me.

I text Larissa back, I'm okay. Thanks for asking. See you at Easter.

I start to draft a new text to Eli, but my fingers hover above my phone, unsure what to type. I settle on a simple, hey.

He doesn't respond.

Chapter 29

The Miserables

SATURDAY

It's a little after ten a.m. I want to go downstairs and get a bowl of cereal, but Mom is in the kitchen and I don't want to run into her. I'm all out of snacks from Mr. Greene.

I'm contemplating ways to sneak to the kitchen and go unnoticed when the doorbell rings, and I hear Reina's voice. I leave my room, tiptoe down the steps, and peek around the living-room corner. Mom, Reina, and Reina's parents are standing in our hallway. Mr. and Mrs. Acosta are frowning, and Reina stands in between them with her arms stiff at her sides, and for some reason she's wearing a navy-blue military jacket with big gold buttons. She drops down and kneels in front of Mom.

"Ms. Pierce, please forgive me," she sings in a low, deep voice. "I lied to you and that was wrong. Please allow me to apologize in song!"

Mom stares at Reina, confused. "Honey . . . what?"

"Get up, Reina," Mrs. Acosta hisses, pulling Reina to her feet. "We told you to apologize, not *sing*."

"Okay, okay. Sorry," Reina says. She gestures at her outfit and explains to Mom, "I'm supposed to be like Javert, the police inspector from *Les Mis*. I thought if I sang my apology to you, you'd really feel the emotion behind it."

Mom stares at her blankly.

"Specifically, I'm like Javert from the movie version with Russell Crowe," Reina continues. "You know, the scene when Javert apologizes to the mayor, Jean Valjean, because he accused him of being a man who once escaped from prison? The funny thing is that Jean Valjean *really is* a man who once escaped from prison. I'd definitely suggest seeing the play live instead of watching the movie, but I guess it—"

"*Reina.*" Mr. Acosta's cheeks are so puffed up and red, his face looks like it's going to explode.

"Sorry!" Reina says. She turns back to Mom. "Ms. Carol, I truly apologize for pretending to be my mom and saying that Chloe was staying at my house when she really wasn't. It was a bad thing to do, and I'm really, really sorry."

Mom nods. "Thank you, Reina. I know you were just trying to help Chloe, but you girls can't go around lying to your parents like this."

"That's exactly what we told her," Mrs. Acosta says, giving Reina a disapproving look.

Reina glances over and sees me peeking around the corner. Her eyes widen.

"Excuse me, Ms. Carol," she says, "can I please use the bathroom?"

"Of course," Mom says.

Reina darts off in my direction. Once she's fully turned the corner, she grabs my hand and pulls me into the bathroom.

"Are you okay?" I whisper. "I called you yesterday, but your dad answered and said you were grounded. I'm so sorry about all of this. I didn't mean for you to get in trouble, too."

"I'm fine," she says. "I mean, the only bad thing is that this morning my mom tried to tell me I couldn't go to prom, but I told her if I couldn't go to prom, she'd better cough up the $350 I spent on my dress."

"Yeah, right. You did *not* say that."

"Yes, I did!" She pauses. "Okay, so I actually said I spent a really long time saving up to buy my dress and it was an important investment, and she's always going on about how I spend money on unnecessary things, like that time I bought a $200 replica of the hat Audrey Hepburn wore in *My Fair Lady*, but it got all smashed and ruined by the time it was delivered. Anyway, I basically asked her not to make me return my first-ever important investment."

"What'd she say after that?"

"Nothing. That's when she took my phone."

I burst into laughter and rush to cover my mouth. It's the first time I've laughed in days.

Reina hisses, "Don't laugh at my misfortune!"

"I'm sorry," I say. "I hope you had a good time at camp, at least."

"Those kids were a nightmare. Everyone thinks they're

the next Jennifer Lawrence or Michael B. Jordan. But who cares about how much I hate being a counselor? I want you to tell me *everything*."

So I do, as quickly as I can. When I reach the part about agreeing to go with Eli to his dad's house, Reina stops me. Slowly, she says, "You like him again, don't you?"

I stare at her. My first instinct is to pretend I don't know who she's talking about. "Who are you talking about?"

"Don't play stupid," she says. *"Eli."*

I wince and take a deep breath. "He's really not as bad as you think."

She snorts. "You don't say."

"Don't get me wrong, he's still annoying, but he can also be really sweet, and he's a lot smarter than most people probably think, and . . . I don't know. It's hard to explain! It just came out of nowhere."

"Has it really come out of nowhere, though?" she asks. "This has been in the works for a long time, if you ask me."

"We kissed," I say.

She smirks. "Is he a good kisser?"

I nod, and she rolls her eyes.

"What?" I say. "I know you don't like him, but I think if you gave him a chance, you'd get along."

"It's not that I don't like him," she says. "It's just that you're my best friend, and if I'm being honest, no one will ever be good enough for you. Not even a young Daniel Day-Lewis, and he's *British* and has *three* Academy Awards."

233

"Who is Daniel DeLewis?"

She jerks back, shocked. "He's only the best actor in . . . never mind." She sighs. "Chloe, you're smart, and I trust your judgment. If you like Eli, I'll support that."

"Thanks." I start to tell her that I haven't heard from him since Thursday, but she's already moving on to the next topic.

"Let's get to the important stuff," she says. "What did your mom say when you told her about the audition? Was she pissed?"

I nod. "If I'm accepted into the conservatory, she's not going to let me go."

"Chloe, I'm so sorry," she says, frowning. "Something good has to come out of all this."

Reina's mom calls her name, and Reina sighs.

"I'd better go before my mom kills me." She hugs me tightly. "If I can find a way to sneak my phone, I'll text you."

I wish I could keep her here with me. Like so many other times, I'm reminded of how grateful I am that she moved into Trey's old house, how grateful I am to have her as a friend.

I follow Reina out into the hallway and peek around the living-room corner, watching as she and her parents leave. I linger too long, and Mom turns and catches me standing there. I spin around and grab some fruit and a big bag of chips from the kitchen before I dash upstairs to my dungeon.

Chapter 30

Resurrection Day

SUNDAY

The bathroom is right above the kitchen, so as I'm doing my hair in the morning before church, I overhear Mom and Jean-Marc talking about me.

"I left Haiti when I was about her age. I turned out okay," Jean-Marc says. "She'll be fine."

"You were not her age. There's a big difference between seventeen and twenty-three," Mom says. "I think I know what's best for my daughter."

Jean-Marc makes a *tsk* sound. "I think you need to have a little more faith in her."

Faith. I repeat this word to myself as I walk downstairs and enter the kitchen. They abruptly stop talking once they see me. Mom and I exchange a stiff good morning.

We pretend to be a happy family as we walk into church wearing our bright pastels. I look innocent in my A-line sundress. Mom and Jean-Marc smile and walk arm in arm. No one would be able to tell that Mom grounded me and we're barely on speaking terms.

Mom always gets emotional at church. Today is no different. As she listens to our pastor, tears linger at the corners of her eyes, and she wipes them away. Usually, I reach out and squeeze her hand, but today I fold my hands in my lap and face forward.

I realize this is probably not what Jesus would do.

Jean-Marc has to work after church, which is unfortunate. I was hoping he'd stick around to act as a buffer between Mom and me. I end up spending most of the day in my room again, while Mom bustles around the kitchen, baking a pie. I ignore my grumbling stomach as the sweet smell of cinnamon apples wafts upstairs. Baking a pie on Easter is something we usually do together. I don't want to care that she didn't ask me to help.

Every so often, I find myself glancing out of my window across the street at Eli's house. Three days ago, he confessed that he liked me. Now I can't even get him to text me back, and I have no idea why. I am *so* not looking forward to having dinner with him and our two angry moms.

I hear a car door slam, and I glance out the window again. I watch as Ms. Linda walks to her front door, carrying grocery bags. She's dressed in all her Easter glory, wearing a bright yellow dress, matching stilettos, and a wide-brimmed hat. A wave of sadness comes over me as I look down at her. Years ago, she was just like me: a young girl with dreams. But things didn't turn out the way she expected. Now she just wants her children to go further than she did, but she doesn't want to listen to what *their* dreams are.

Which brings me back to Mom and how we see things so differently. Will we ever be able to understand each other?

A couple hours later, Mom yells, "Chloe, are you ready? It's time to go."

Reluctantly, I trudge out of my room and steel myself for quite possibly the worst evening ever.

With one hand holding a pie and the other placed on her hip, Mom says, "I'd prefer for us to stay home, because I think you and Eli have seen enough of each other, but Linda is looking forward to this dinner, and it would break her heart if we didn't go." She narrows her eyes. "Behave yourself."

Behave myself. She really means: don't talk to Eli.

"Okay," I say.

As we head across the street, I glance up at Eli's bedroom window, and his light is off. Maybe he ended up staying at his dad's for Easter. Right now, that doesn't sound like such a bad thing.

When Ms. Linda answers the door, she and Mom hug each other, and Ms. Linda fusses over the fact that Mom baked a pie, like she doesn't bake one every time we come over for dinner. My welcome isn't as warm.

"Well, hello, Miss Thing," she says, giving me a stiff hug. "Heard you've had quite the week."

What am I supposed to say to that? I just stand there awkwardly until she ushers us inside.

Larissa is already seated at the dining-room table. I hurry to grab the empty seat next to her so I won't have to sit beside Mom. Larissa hugs me when I sit down.

"I like your outfit," I say, taking in her black skater dress and Doc Martens.

"Thanks," she says. "My mom doesn't."

Mom sits across the table beside Ms. Linda. There's no sign of Eli. I'm torn between relief and disappointment.

Even though I'd rather not be here, I can't deny that the food looks amazing. Baked chicken, macaroni and cheese, sweet potatoes, and collard greens. I haven't eaten a real meal in days. I'm wondering what I'm going to put on my plate first, when I hear the sound of Geezer's feet trotting down the steps. He makes his way into the dining room, and seconds later he's followed by Eli.

Our eyes lock as he walks to the table. I wish he could read my mind, because all I'm thinking is, *Where the heck did you disappear to?* He opens his mouth like he might say something to me, but Ms. Linda speaks first.

"I told you that dog isn't allowed in my dining room, Elijah," she says.

Eli abruptly stops and then backpedals, leading Geezer into the kitchen and locking him behind his dog gate. When he returns, he sits down next to his mom, directly across from me.

"Nice of you to join us," Ms. Linda says, frowning at him. "We can't say grace without you."

He mumbles an apology and pulls uncomfortably at the collar of his button-up. He looks at me again, but averts his eyes when Mom loudly clears her throat. I glance at her, and she's frowning at Eli *hard*, like it's taking all of her effort not to yell at him.

So, dinner, of course, is very awkward. I spend the next half hour trying to catch Eli's eye again, but he avoids looking at me. Mom and Ms. Linda are the only ones making conversation. At one point, Larissa squeezes my hand under the table. It's nice to know there's someone here who is on my side.

Ms. Linda brings out Mom's pie, and over dessert, Mom asks Larissa about her classes. When Larissa is done answering her, Ms. Linda says, "Eli also has some college news."

Eli glances at his mom and frowns. He pulls at his collar again.

"Mom," Larissa says, almost like a warning.

Ignoring her, Ms. Linda explains, "Eli isn't going to UNC anymore. He'll be going to art school in San Francisco instead."

"Seriously?" I say. Eli finally looks at me again and nods. At first, I'm elated, but then I'm disappointed that this is how I'm finding out and that he didn't tell me himself.

"Wow," Mom says, surprised. "Well, congratulations, Eli."

"Thank you," he says.

"It's not pre-law, that's for sure," Ms. Linda adds. "But, who knows, after he outgrows this phase, maybe he'll come back around to it."

"It's not a *phase*," Eli says.

"Baby, I'm just telling it like it is."

Eli suddenly stands up. "I need some fresh air."

"Now, just wait one second," Ms. Linda says. "Remember what we talked about. You can't leave this table until you apologize to Ms. Carol for taking Chloe with you on your little expedition."

"Wait, what?" I say.

Eli's shoulders sag. He looks at the floor and says nothing.

Mom sighs. "He doesn't have to apologize, Linda. Chloe already told me everything was her idea."

"Oh, come on, Carol," Ms. Linda says, shaking her head. "We both know that's not true."

"It is true," I say, growing unnerved by the dejected look on Eli's face. "Eli didn't have anything to do with it."

"I honestly expected a little more from you, sweetie," Ms. Linda says, turning her attention to me. "You're smarter than this. How could you let Eli get you in so much trouble?"

I blink, stunned at her words. When I finally find my voice, it's full of anger. "He didn't do anything wrong."

Eli doesn't bother to defend himself. He stares silently at the floor, clenching his jaw.

"Who wants some more pie?" Larissa asks, with a forced smile.

Mom stands up, too. "Eli, you don't need to apologize to me. My issue lies with my daughter. Chloe, get your things. I think it's time for us to go."

"Eli, apologize right now," Ms. Linda says. "Do not embarrass me."

"Not everything is about you!" Eli snaps.

Now Ms. Linda is on her feet. "Who do you think you're talking to like that?"

"Please stop arguing," Larissa begs. "Can everyone just sit down?"

"Ms. Carol, I'm sorry for asking Chloe to drive me to my dad's," Eli says. He looks at me. "I'm sorry, Chlo. Really."

And then he rushes out of the room, leaving Geezer to bark wildly from behind his dog gate.

"Eli, wait." I get up and follow him outside to his car. He turns around, and every bit of anger I held toward him evaporates. He looks so tired and sad.

Softly, I say, "Why have you been ghosting me? Why didn't you let me know when you got back?"

He shakes his head. "Chloe, I meant everything I said to you the other night at my dad's, but I don't think—"

He doesn't have a chance to finish his sentence, because Ms. Linda storms outside and tells him that he'd better not go anywhere. Eli asks if she can please just give him some space, and they go back and forth until they're practically shouting at each other. Larissa runs outside and puts herself in between them.

"Mom, just let him go," she says.

Eli doesn't wait to hear if Ms. Linda will agree. He hops in his car, reverses into the street, and drives away.

"Can you believe him?" Ms. Linda asks, looking exhausted.

"He'll be back," Larissa says. "You know he will. He's just upset. You both are."

"But he has no reason to be upset with me," Ms. Linda says. "I'm the one who convinced your father he should pay for Eli to go to art school. Don't you think I know how gifted my son is? Even though I want more for him, I'm still agreeing to let him go. Why am *I* the bad guy?"

Larissa puts her arm around her mother. "Come on, let's go in the house."

Quietly, they walk up the driveway and head back inside. Minutes later, Mom appears in the doorway, holding what's left of her pie.

"I think we'd better go home," she says to me.

We silently walk across the street. I spare one last glance down the block, looking for Eli's car. I wish he'd finished his sentence. Now I'll spend the rest of the night wondering what he was going to say. Wondering if it was going to be something good . . .

Or something bad.

Chapter 31

A Philosophy

Later, I call Eli and it goes straight to voicemail. I want to know if he's okay. And why he apologized to Mom for bringing me to North Carolina when it wasn't his fault. Why he apologized to *me*.

I flop onto my bed, and once again find myself staring up at my Avery Johnson poster. When I did this a week ago, I felt so hopeful. Now everything is ruined.

The photo of my dad holding me catches my eye. I stare at the broad smile on his face and wonder how different my life would be if he never died. Would he allow me to go to the conservatory if I was accepted? Maybe I wouldn't have had to sneak away to audition because he would have gladly taken me.

I guess I'll never know.

Eli thinks that everything happens for a reason. But I have a hard time understanding this philosophy. People lose loved ones; they get broken bones and broken hearts. They have lifelong dreams crushed in a matter of seconds. What are the reasons for that?

I feel like Princess Aurora in the ballet, *The Sleeping Beauty*. She was just trying to enjoy her birthday party, and then she pricked her finger on a spindle and slept for a hundred years until Prince Désiré came along and woke her up with a kiss. What we have in common is that we had bigger plans for our lives, but then we got locked away against our will. The difference is that, despite what Eli said, I don't think anyone is coming to save me.

So I'll have to save myself.

I hop up and open my door, planning to walk straight into Mom's room, but she's already standing in the doorway. I blink at her, surprised.

"I was going to say good night," she says.

"I was actually coming to talk to you, too," I say.

"Can I say what I have to say first?"

I nod and take in a deep breath, waiting.

"When you were younger and had nightmares, you and I had a routine," she says. "I'd hear you rustling around in your bed, then I'd hear your little feet padding down the hall. You'd stop at the foot of my bed, and I'd open my eyes and you'd be standing right there, waiting for me to wake up. Then you'd climb up beside me, and I'd convince you that your nightmares weren't real. You'd fall asleep after about ten minutes. You remember that?"

I nod again, thinking of how her calm voice used to soothe me back to sleep.

"I had no idea what I was doing," she says. "I was raising you by myself, but I knew that as long as I kept you safe, I was doing something right. It felt like it was us against the world. It still feels that way sometimes." She looks down and smiles softly to herself. Then she lifts her eyes to meet mine. "I know you love ballet and that this conservatory could open a lot of doors for you, but I'm not comfortable with you being all the way in New York City."

"But Mom—"

She holds up her hand. "Let me finish. You think I don't want to let you go because I think something bad will happen to you, like your father. He wasn't a careful person, and when I look at you, it's true that I'm reminded all the time that I could lose you, too, just as easily. But that's not why I don't want to let you go. I know you're careful, and intelligent, and capable of being on your own. I just thought I'd have you here a little longer. I wasn't expecting to give you up to the world just yet. This all took me by surprise, and I let my feelings get in the way of considering what was best for you. That wasn't fair."

I stare at her and continue to listen, waiting anxiously for what she'll say next.

"So, if you're accepted into the conservatory, you have my permission to go," she says. "And I'll support whatever decision you make even if you don't get in. Whether that's to move to New York after graduation, or if you want to try something else."

I freeze and replay her words to make sure I understood correctly. "Are you serious?"

"Yes," she says.

I kind of just stare at her in disbelief. Then my words come in a torrent. "Thank you, Mom," I say, hugging her. "Thank you. Thank you. Thank you."

She wraps her arms around me, and I marvel at how much I'd misunderstood her all this time.

"I'm so sorry for bringing up my dad like that the other night," I say. "I really didn't—"

"It's all right, baby," she says softly. "To be honest, he probably would have been proud of the adventure you had."

I hug her tighter. I've never thought about how much I'll miss her, too. It really has been just us for so long. My heart sinks at the realization that a time will eventually come when I won't see her every day.

"No matter what ends up happening, I promise I'll always make time to visit you," I tell her. "And I'll call every day."

"You'd better," she says. She pulls away and gives me a stern look. "But you're still grounded. No car for a month. You hear me?"

"Yes, ma'am." I'm so happy I don't even care. I could walk to school for the rest of the year and still not care.

"You'd better get to sleep," she says. "Back to school for you, tomorrow."

"Wait," I say, as she turns toward her room. "I'm sorry that your vacation ended early, and that you had to come home to so much chaos. Did you at least have a good time?"

She smiles. "I did. Honestly, I was a little upset when Jean-Marc got sick because I wasn't ready to leave yet. I haven't relaxed like that in a long time. I need to do it more often."

"I hope you do," I say.

In another version of Mom's life, maybe she isn't a nurse or a widow. She's a thrill seeker or an adventuress. Maybe I'm not even her daughter, and she has the freedom to travel the world according to her whims. We'll never know.

But this is what I know about the life she lives now: she is my mother, and I am her daughter. We're not perfect or trying to be. But we're trying to understand each other better.

I hug her again, and this time she laughs.

"What was that for?" she asks.

"Just because I love you."

She smooths her hand over my hair like she used to do all those times when I'd climb into her bed, seeking refuge from my nightmares. "I love you, too."

❦

I'm lying in bed, once again staring up at my poster of Avery Johnson. I'm thinking about the philosophy that everything happens for a reason, and that maybe there is more truth to it than I thought.

If Mom didn't take those extra seconds to run upstairs to get her makeup bag, then Eli wouldn't have had time to catch me and ask for a ride. And if we didn't have our accident, I wouldn't have gone to the audition in North Carolina, which means I wouldn't have reconnected with Trey and Larissa. Maybe I wouldn't have bumped into Avery Johnson in the hallway. As strange as it sounds, maybe even my injury happened for a reason. It's the starting point that set off this chain of events. And, finally, if this trip never happened, Eli and I would be in a completely different place.

I don't know what he was going to say to me, but I'm not going to wait around until he's ready. Knowing him, it could take a year and a half. If I want to talk, I'll have to find him. And that's exactly what I'm going to do.

Chapter 32

Pas De Deux

MONDAY

I dream that I'm looking for Eli in school, but the entire building is empty. I keep walking through the hall, searching and searching, but there's no sign of him.

It seems like my dream has become reality when I notice that his car isn't in his driveway when I leave for school in the morning. I don't see him in the hallways, either. Part of me hopes he'll find me at my locker, just like the day he gave me the sketch of my face, but it doesn't happen.

"Have you seen Eli around?" I ask Reina later in the cafeteria as we're standing in the lunch line.

"Nope," she says, scowling at the meatball subs in front of us. "Whether or not there's actual meat in these meatballs is questionable." She turns to me. "What kind of lunch do you think they'll have at the conservatory?"

"I don't know," I say, looking around the cafeteria like Eli might materialize out of nowhere. "I don't even know if I got in."

Reina pulls on my shirtsleeve to get my attention. "Relax, Chlo. Maybe he got caught smoking in the courtyard again and has in-school suspension. I'm sure he'll find you after school so you guys can suck face." She sticks her finger in her mouth, like the thought of us kissing makes her want to puke.

I laugh and shake my head. "You're so dramatic."

"Maybe, but you love me anyway."

We spend the rest of lunch looking at Reina's shoe options for prom again. Her dress is strapless and red satin, old-Hollywood style. Eventually, she calls over her date, Greg, and makes him weigh in, too. When the bell rings and we're filing out of the cafeteria, Reina says, "You sure you don't want to go to prom with me and Greg? I swear we won't be *those people* who pack on the PDA. We'll probably only make out in the limo, like, once or twice."

I start to say no, but it's silly to think that every school-dance experience will be bad just because I had an unfortunate accident trying to get to Homecoming. Like with everything else, maybe I need to give prom a chance, too.

"I'll think about it," I say.

⁂

I find Eli in the art room after school. I don't know why I didn't think to look here earlier.

He's the only one in the room, and he's sitting close to an easel, sketching with the utmost concentration. He's wearing big noise-canceling headphones, and his back is angled toward the door, so he doesn't hear me as I walk in. And he doesn't hear me as I creep closer to him, trying to get a better view of what he's drawing.

I make out the shape of a girl's body. She's in mid-leap, her legs outstretched like she's soaring through the sky. Her arms are in arabesque, and her expression is serene. She looks strong and confident, ready to conquer the world one leap at a time.

It takes me a minute to realize that this girl is me. This is the drawing he was hesitant to show me in the St. Maria dance studio. But this is much larger than the page in his sketchbook.

I gasp in awe, and it's loud enough to finally make him turn around.

Shocked, he drops his pencil and it clatters to the floor. "Shit," he says, eyes wide. "What are you doing in here?"

I don't answer him. I'm still staring at the drawing. I step forward to get a closer look at the details. He even added the scar on my right forearm and the scar on my ankle, peeking out between my ribbons.

"This is beautiful," I say. I look at him. He has dark circles around his eyes, and I wonder if he got any sleep last night. "It's me, isn't it?"

He stares at me for a moment, then nods.

"It's amazing," I tell him.

He doesn't say anything. He looks at the drawing and shrugs a little. "Thanks."

"Sorry," I say, picking up on his hesitancy. I realize how invasive I'm being right now. I take a step back. "I know you didn't want me to see this yet."

"It's for my senior project," he says. He walks over and opens one of the lockers on the far side of the room and pulls out large sheets of paper. He spreads them out on the desks.

They're more drawings of people. The first is of Trey driving in his Jeep, laughing. One hand is on the wheel and another is moving through his dreads. The next one is of Geezer lying in the grass by the reflecting pool in D.C. Then there's one of Larissa and Will slow dancing in Will's backyard, and there's a drawing of Will and his roommates gathered around the television playing a video game. The last drawing is his dad carrying his fishing rod and bait. He's giving a thumbs-up.

"This is the story I'm choosing to tell," Eli explains.

I glance back at the unfinished drawing of me on the easel. "Have you been working on these all day?"

"Yeah."

We stare down at the drawings and fall silent for a moment.

"Why did you stop responding to my messages?" I ask. "You can't just shut me out like that instead of talking to me. It's the same thing you did before."

"I know, and I'm sorry," he says. "After you left my dad's house, my mom called me, and she was pissed that I took you with me. She said that I had no business getting you in trouble like that, and I realized she was right."

"So you thought you'd just ignore me instead of saying something?" I ask, annoyed. "What kind of response is that?"

"A stupid one, I know. But, regardless, you could do a lot better than me. That's what I was trying to tell you last night."

I blink at him. "*That's* what you wanted to tell me? What does that even mean?"

"Come on, Chlo," he says. "You don't lie. You don't get in trouble, and last week was the first time you did either of those things. I'm a bad influence."

"I lied to my mom before I even knew you'd end up coming with me."

"I crashed your car," he says. "I blackmailed you into giving me a ride. Who does shit like that? Shitty people, that's who."

"Well, the blackmail was messed up," I agree. "But crashing my car was an accident. You only did that because I threw up!"

He starts pacing the room in that fidgety way of his. "I don't know," he says. "We have the rest of spring and summer. Cool. But in the fall, you could be in New York City if you get into that dance school, and I'll be in San Francisco. It won't last."

My stomach clenches. "What happened to us visiting each other?"

He stops pacing and looks at me. "We say that now, but we both know it probably won't happen. You might be too busy dancing, and you could meet some ballet guy, who's, like, a New York City trust-fund baby or some shit, and he'll sweep you off your feet, *literally*, and you'll forget about me."

He starts pacing again.

I've seen a lot of different versions of Eli these past few days, but this is a new one: insecure.

I step forward and stand in front of him. I put my hand on his chest, so he'll stop pacing. I can feel his heart beating beneath my palm. "It's true we don't know what's going to happen, but the best things happen when we don't plan them out. Like our whole trip. Like with you and me."

"I don't know," he repeats. He shakes his head and looks away.

I lower my hand and link it with his. At first his fingers are limp, but then they wrap around mine.

"We can worry about the fall when it gets here," I say. "Plus, one time this boy told me that everything happens for a reason. So we should just relax."

His expression softens. "Sounds like a smart guy."

I shrug. "Ehh, I guess he's kind of smart."

"And funny."

"Less funny than he thinks."

He begins to smile. "But is he handsome?"

"Oh yeah. *Very* good-looking."

He flashes his white teeth. "Oh really?"

I nod. "Really."

He puts his hand on my waist and pulls me closer. I take in his familiar scent.

"I'm sorry for being stupid," he says.

"It's okay," I say. "Just don't do it again."

He leans down, and I close my eyes, waiting for him to kiss me. I feel his lips hovering over mine, but they don't make contact.

I open my eyes. He's looking at me with his wolfish grin. "What are you doing?" I whisper.

"For the record, if some dancer guy tries to steal you, I'll fly there and kick his ass."

I laugh and shake my head. "Stop it."

"For real. I'll—"

I kiss him so he'll be quiet.

Chapter 33

Message

From: Jeffrey Baptiste [jeffreybaptiste@averyjohnson.org]

Sent: Thursday, May 9, 2019, 2:11 p.m.

To: Chloe Pierce [cpierce17@gmail.com]

Subject: Avery Johnson Dance Conservatory Decision Letter

Dear Ms. Pierce:

We were impressed with your dancing at the Raleigh, North Carolina, audition . . .

Chapter 34

Promenade

MAY

Here's something you should know about me: I'm going to the Junior-Senior Prom.

"Come get in the picture, Chlo," Reina says.

We're standing on my front lawn, taking pictures as we wait for the limo. Reina is a knockout in her dress. When Greg first saw her, his pale cheeks turned the same color as his matching red vest.

I'm wearing a strapless, violet, floor-length chiffon dress, with silver sequins sewn into the bodice and on the hem. It was the first dress I tried on at the store, and I loved it so much I didn't need to see any other options. Larissa was so excited when I told her I was going to prom that she came home to do my hair and makeup. About an hour ago, she twisted my hair into an intricate topknot that I'll never be able to replicate and applied shimmer to my eyelids and cheekbones.

Mom, Mr. and Mrs. Acosta, and Greg's parents take

what feels like a billion pictures of us. Mom takes a couple pictures of me by myself. I send one to Trey and he sends back a bunch of heart-eyes emojis. Then he sends a picture of him and Eric wearing matching tuxes because their prom is tonight, too. We have plans to meet up this weekend at the beach.

"You look so beautiful, baby," Mom says, sniffling a little.

"Thanks, Mom," I say, hugging her.

"I'm so proud of you," she says.

She's been telling me this almost every day since I got my e-mail from the conservatory. I was wait-listed. At first, I was devastated. The moment where I slipped during the audition showed up in my dreams over and over again. It was a really hard e-mail to read. But I'm at the top of the waitlist, so there's a chance that someone could drop out at the last minute or choose another conservatory, and then the spot will be mine. Either way, I'm not giving up on my dream. I'll never regret everything I went through in order to audition, and I'll still move to New York City after graduation. There's a place for me in the ballet world somewhere. I know that to be true.

Our limo finally pulls up in front of the house. It's white and shiny like it just went through a car wash.

Reina looks at me and frowns. *Where's your date?* she mouths.

I ask myself the same question and pull my phone out of my clutch to find the answer. Then the Greenes' front door swings open and Larissa runs outside.

"He's coming! Don't leave yet!" she shouts, turning around and beckoning for someone to follow her.

Eli steps onto the front porch and adjusts his tie. He's wearing a slim-cut black tux, and his hair is starting to grow back, so his curls are nice and trimmed. There are so many different shades of purple that it's easy to confuse another shade for violet, so I suggested that I go with him to pick out his vest and tie. Very offended, he told me, "I can pick out a tie, Chlo, sheesh. Give me some credit, please." He was right. His vest and tie are the exact shade of my dress.

He strides across the street, sporting his confident smile. He hugs Mom and says hello to the other parents and slides my corsage onto my wrist. It has violets and a white ribbon.

"Yes, I picked it out myself," he says, still smiling. "You look really beautiful."

"Thank you. You don't look too bad yourself."

I kiss his cheek. He's wearing cologne with a chypre scent. And there's no lingering tobacco smell. He hasn't smoked a cigarette in almost three weeks. He still hates the patch, though.

I pin on his boutonniere, and then we take more pictures as a group. Larissa buzzes around Eli and me, touching up my hair and trying to smooth out his lapels, but she eventually stops when she realizes she's photobombing all the pictures. Then, at Eli's request, Larissa goes to get Geezer so he can be in our pictures, too.

Right before we get in the limo, Ms. Linda pulls into her driveway and hurries across the street to take a few pictures of Eli and me. She's still coming around to the idea of Eli going to art school. Every now and then she'll make an off-hand comment about how he'd be better off at UNC, but she's stopped trying to argue with him about it. The other day he caught her browsing the San Francisco Art Institute's homepage when she thought he wasn't home.

We climb into the limo, and I'm surprised to see it has a bar. But it's stocked with Coca-Cola and ginger ale since we're under twenty-one.

Greg pulls a little vodka nip out of his pocket. "Anyone want some?"

Eli laughs. "No thanks, bro."

Reina says, "Uh, maybe we should wait to drink until *after* prom is over."

"Okay." Greg shrugs and drops the nip back in his pocket. I hope our vice principal doesn't see it when he's check-ing everyone at the door.

Reina looks at me wide-eyed. The expression on her face says, *What the heck?* I try to hold in my laughter.

I made a special prom playlist, so I plug up my phone to the aux cord, and my go-to girl, Beyoncé, blares through the speakers. Reina jumps up and starts dancing. Eli groans, pre-tending to be annoyed. Then he puts his arm around me and smiles.

Every single moment between us has led up to this one.

It all happened for a reason, just like he said. I can't wait to see what moments the future holds. Who knows. Maybe tonight could be the best night of my life.

Eli lightly brushes his fingers over the shimmer on my cheekbones. "I hope this dance isn't corny," he says.

"It won't be," I say.

He raises an eyebrow. "How do you know?"

I smile and shrug as I lean into him. "I just have a feeling."

Chloe's Prom Playlist

1. "Party"—Beyoncé feat. André 3000

2. "Rather Be"—Clean Bandit feat. Jess Glynne

3. "Int'l Players Anthem (I Choose You)"—UGK feat. OutKast

4. "Uptown Funk"—Mark Ronson feat. Bruno Mars

5. "Candy"—Cameo

6. "Latch"—Disclosure feat. Sam Smith

7. "Square Biz" —Teena Marie

8. "We Found Love"—Calvin Harris feat. Rihanna

9. "Nice for What"—Drake

10. "Hey Ya!"—OutKast

11. "Swag Surfin'"—F.L.Y. (Fast Life Yungstaz)

12. "King of the Dancehall"—Beenie Man

13. "I Would Die 4 U"—Prince

14. "Bougie Party"—Chloe x Halle

Author's Note

I fell in love with dance when I was eight years old. At the time, I had no formal training. My friends and I made up routines for fun. We performed in our town's annual Fourth of July parade every year and were members of our school's dance team. Eventually, my mom signed me up for ballet classes, and I took to the dance form immediately. I loved the precision of it, the required discipline. To me, a ballerina was the ultimate dancer.

There is a moment in this book when Chloe recalls looking at herself in the studio mirror while standing next to her peers, and she has the startling realization that her body type is different from theirs. I experienced a similar moment when I was seventeen. In most cases, I was the only Black girl in my classes. It didn't actively bother me when I was younger, but I found myself feeling frustrated about it toward the end of high school. At that point, I was beginning to fall out of

15. "Wobble"—V.I.C.

16. "Last Dance"—Donna Summer

17. "Adorn"—Miguel

18. "Crazy in Love"—Beyoncé feat. Jay Z

19. "Hold On, We're Going Home"—Drake

20. "Forever Mine"—Andra Day

The End

love with ballet, and I was finding a new love in writing. I cut back on dance classes and focused on enjoying the rest of my senior year. In the fall, I started college as a writing major. But part of me always wondered—and still wonders—what would have happened if I'd stuck with ballet a little longer, pursued it a little harder. Years later, when I wanted to write a book about a girl who was so devoted to one passion she'd risk anything and everything to pursue it, it only made sense to make her passionate about ballet.

Chloe's idol, Avery Johnson, is loosely based on Alvin Ailey and his legacy. When I began working on this book, six years had passed since I stepped foot in a ballet studio. I knew that in order to properly recapture the feeling, I would need to take classes again. I lived in New York City, so what better place to take classes than at Alvin Ailey's Ailey Extension program? I realized right away that I was pretty rusty. I messed up on simple steps and compared what had become my subpar technique to the technique of the dancers around me, who clearly hadn't taken such a long hiatus. I often felt nervous, overwhelmed, and doubtful. But I'm thankful for those feelings because they brought me much closer to Chloe and her feelings of inadequacy after her injury. And, like Chloe, I realized just how much I still loved ballet. I couldn't believe I'd gone so many years without it.

For additional research, I read *Life in Motion: An Unlikely Ballerina* by Misty Copeland and *Taking Flight: From War*

Orphan to Star Ballerina by Michaela DePrince. I'm grateful for their stories and for what these two women represent for young Black ballerinas everywhere.

In real life, ballet conservatories begin holding auditions much earlier in the year, but for the timing of this story, I chose to have auditions in April. Spring is a time for new beginnings, and it's also a time for love. Both of which are so very important to Chloe's story.